The Janeites

Praise for *Nicolas Freeling:*

'Freeling is not merely a great British crime writer, but a great European novelist. At a time when much detective fiction is literary junk food, it's easy to forget that many of the greatest novelists – Dickens, Stendhal, Dostoevsky, Conrad, Victor Hugo – were also crime writers. Like them, Nicolas Freeling recognises that yearning and despair, love and death, are the essence of both crime and art' – Francis Wheen

'Freeling has made the realm of EuroCrime his own' – *Observer*

'Here is an author who is as much concerned with the impulses and motives of the human heart as he is with the details of detection. The combination of elegant style and the continually interesting narrative give his novels their special flavour' – P.D. James

'*The Village Book* is always entertaining – like Freeling's most recent novel *Some Day Tomorrow*, as perceptive a picture as you are likely to encounter of the impact of age and illness on the male psyche. The two can profitably be read side by side, as a prelude to publication of Freeling's 38th novel, *The Janeites*' – Vivienne Menkes-Ivry, *Independent*

'Freeling's whimsical and atmospheric style is here in force, along with his personal asides on the trivia of our existence . . . a rather special book' – Patricia Highsmith

'A major novelist of crime' – *New York Times*

'The mantle of Simenon seems to have been inherited by Nicolas Freeling. His Inspector Van der Valk – less rugged than Rebus, less parsonical than Dalgliesh, more Morse than Frost, and more Maigret than any of them – has become known as a placid but shrewd Dutch bourgeois with an interesting wife; at some point he metamorphosed into Inspector Henri Castang. Marvellous' – Anita Brookner, *Spectator*

'Strongly reminiscent of Simenon. For my taste Freeling is far more vital and colourful' – *San Francisco Chronicle*

'Freeling is the only British novelist of consequence to have tackled modern Europe. I have no doubt this expatriate Englishman joins Graham Greene and George V. Higgins as one of the great crime writers' – Grey Gowrie, *Daily Telegraph*

'*Some Day Tomorrow* is a subtle, sympathetic study of old age and sexual desire. A perfect choice to launch Arcadia's Euro Crime series. May all their follow-ups be as successful' – Philip Purser, *Literary Review*

'I can cheerfully recommend Nicolas Freeling's novels to anyone who enjoys the seriously good crime novel. It is unimaginable that he should ever tell a dull story, and he writes with a warmth and sensitivity all too rare in the genre. Whether he is working on a case for Inspector Van der Valk or creating a complex modern crime novel, the true mystery is always the mystery of the human heart. Intelligent, worldly wise and humane – that is the distinctive voice of Nicolas Freeling' – Lesley Grant-Adamson

Nicolas Freeling is the author of 37 highly acclaimed crime novels and, most recently, *The Village Book: Memoirs*, *Some Day Tomorrow* and *Because of the Cats*, all published by Arcadia. He is the winner of the Golden Dagger Award from the Crime Writers' Association, the Grand Prix de Roman Policier and the Edgar Allan Poe Award of the Mystery Writers of America. He lives in Grandfontaine, France.

The Janeites

NICOLAS FREELING

A

ARCADIA BOOKS

LONDON

Arcadia Books Ltd
15–16 Nassau Street
London W1W 7AB

www.arcadiabooks.co.uk

First published in the United Kingdom 2002
Copyright © Nicolas Freeling 2002

A catalogue record for this book is available from the British Library

ISBN 1-900850-73-7

Typeset in Ehrhardt by Northern Phototypesetting Co. Ltd, Bolton
Printed in the United Kingdom by Bell & Bain Ltd, Glasgow

Arcadia Books' distributors are as follows:

in the UK and elsewhere in Europe:
Turnaround Publishers Services
Unit 3, Olympia Trading Estate
Coburg Road
London N22 6TZ

in the US and Canada:
Consortium Book Sales and Distribution
1045 Westgate Drive
St Paul, MN 55114-1065

in Australia:
Tower Books
PO Box 213
Brookvale NSW 2100

in New Zealand:
Addenda
Box 78224
Grey Lynn
Auckland

in South Africa:
Quartet Sales and Marketing
PO Box 1218
Northcliffe
Johannesburg 2115

Introduction

In the plain, there are too many people.

There are too many little roads which bump into one another. Because of this too many cars had also bumped into one another, and the Authority had spent a great deal of money making round-abouts: there were too many of these. Likewise signposts, pointing to places. Our dear Alsace; Oberhausbergen and Niederhausbergen (which nobody can ever find.) Well, in England they've a Nether Wallop and a Middle Wallop. Ray turned the car to the right anyhow; it was time to climb out of this dense world.

Fields began to slope, and there were vines on them. Ray's spirits rose with the road: fresher air up here and there were hills in front of him. It was a fine autumn day and the grapes needed all the sun they could get. He had been told to 'look for the castle': the road made a kink and there was the castle, across a valley and perched up on the scarp; charming remnant of a robber baron's fortress.

He came to the village and this was good, too. Not picturesque enough to be a tourist attraction, but some shapely old houses, and a Renaissance fountain for horses to drink from, and a pretty church early enough to be pre-Gothic. There was also a thirteenth-century old man smoking a pipe and sunning himself on a doorstep. His attitude said that labouring in the vineyard was for others.

"Perhaps you know William Barton?" The sun was hot: the old gentleman wore a leather jacket buttoned up to the neck, and woolly carpet-slippers, and a woolly cap of equally violent check, with a pompom. The countrymen no longer wear berets much.

"*Ouais.*"

"You could tell me the way?" There was a bit of wondering whether this information were not too precious to part with.

"*Ouais.*" Took the pipe to point with. It wasn't even complicated.

That way was the Château but a ways before that you turn, see, and there's a track going up, quite steep and doesn't go anywhere but it takes you there. Which it did too. Sharp up, and round some well-cared-for vines, and there was a gate, and a house built on the steepest of the meadow. Spectacular view, much like that of the castle further along – monarch of all it surveys – of the vineyards and the valley further down and the plain beyond, across to distant hills and the sunlight playing on the whole. Clouds were blowing up from the west. Ray had been wondering why this William lived in such an out-of-the-way corner; the situation explained some things. Modern house, quite big; splendid terrace on the far side, overhanging the drop. Plenty of room for garden (planned but nothing much done yet) and below that a drystone wall and the big sweep of vines. All this had cost a lot of money.

A big man answered the door; tall and broad, with the look of the athlete: large open face, handsome, and smooth brown hair.

"Apologies; I was looking for Mr Barton."

"Found him, too. Man selling, due for disappointment."

"Psst – they're giving it away."

"So they can't get rid of it. Even up here it's what I don't want."

"Name of Marquis help at all?"

"You voting for him or he voting for you?"

"Said that Bill's the man to see."

"Now tell me what he really said."

"Said you were a thorough swine. Now would you like to give something for the widows and the orphans?" The meaningless citified talk – Ray is used to that, can do it too. He got a slow smile.

"You better come in, it's wet on the doorstep. You like a beer?"

"Place like this and there's no champagne?"

"Siddown where I can see you. Now tell me. Cop you're not, so who are you?"

"Name of Ray, I'm just a friend."

"Of the Marquis; a real close friend. And he told you, Bill was eager to get enrolled?"

"No, I only like girls."

"And you've come all the way from Paris, talk the language and everything."

"Yes, a clever little dick; I'm a Jesuit."

"Good christ, you're a curé."

"They've threatened me with that a time or two – told them I wouldn't be good at it."

"That Marquis, I'll eat his balls."

"Better not, he might need them."

"A Jesuit – ho, a hard man. Intellectual."

"Got a hard God – otherwise no more than you."

"What are you doing out here?"

"William – silly question. What are you doing? Scratching your arse."

"That's right, I'm retired. Cruise liner, deckchair, swimming-pool here inna basement."

"No future in that. Chess, gardening, give you an interest. Green Party maybe, for when the nuclear power goes critical."

"You sit there, while I get the champagne." It was a strange room, well designed but oddly bare. Some bits of nice furniture, clean but it didn't look lived in.

"Take hold, curé. Here's to us, salud y pesetas."

"You listen, now. I ran across the Marquis, he tells me ol' Bill, here in this house, writing notices saying Achtung Minen! and sticking them round the shop. Asks me to look him up, he's a nice chap. I plod out here in the bushes, you call me Curé."

"I'm suspicious by nature. And by training. Sit outside here with the shotgun across the knee like Duke Mantee. What do you want – to convert me?"

"No no no, I've got more respect for you than that. Tickets for the prayer-meeting I don't have. Be a Buddhist or a Moonie I don't care. But planted there, saying Fuck You, I'm fireproof – that gets up my nose. You ain't. You're crossing the road, comes some prick on a motorbike, you're in a little trolley, where's my legs. Man, the holy nuns are looking after people like you, cup of tisane and a pill at bed-time." William filled both glasses, drank his off, meditated.

"I got a cancer, Marky tell you that?"

"He did; I'm not just a Jesuit, I'm a doctor. At that, pretty good."

"Curé – I'll call you Ray, okay? I'm planning to be what they call a Stoic."

"No bad idea. Be a bit of an Epicure too, maybe, let's not disdain pleasures?"

"My wife left me; was that on the news too? I didn't take very kindly to getting all these items in a row, either."

"Let's be serious." Ray reached for the bottle to see what was left. "I'm no great expert on wives, myself I haven't any. The crab is a tricky animal, there I'm something of an expert; we play chess together. You're a young man and an athlete, mentally you feel defeated; that gives him an unfair advantage. Sit moping in the corner, that's like giving him a pawn. You tell me who diagnosed you, what treatment he prescribed, I can look up all the technical dossier, think about a ploy. I win these games as often as not. Upon that note, let's go out and have lunch; there are some goodish places as they tell me. If I may say so you're looking like a fellow who opens a tin of baked beans."

"Whirl of bloody gaiety, are you?" siad William getting up.

"I don't have a consulting room. Work at the research institute. So a restaurant is as good a place as any, for listening to stories. While picking at the piece of fish. . . A Porsche, yet. I come visiting in a tin can, drive away in this."

"Yes; where I come from we were pretty well paid."

In the business, Dr Valdez is also widely known as Boogie Acetoso. These comics from Argentina (reading matter in research institutes will often startle the innocent onlooker) are violent – for sure – and vulgar, very: so after all is the crab. In Spanish 'El Accitoso' – the greasy one – could be rendered pedantically as 'nobody gets a grip on him'. Ray is no Superman but like Boogie he has a talent for win-ning. In the research world, where they seek to get a grip on the crab, he is not thought of as an unusual technician. The Oncology people hold him in respect because he has a talent betimes thought uncanny: he can often outguess them when the crab – a champion at this game – looks to be winning. In plain terms he has brought off spectacular results, exercising 'alternative medicine': a sniffy phrase which 'school-doctors' often pronounce, and they mean it pejoratively.

Dr Valdez drove home thinking, to be quite honest, about cars: the little Renault Four had been greatly beloved and so, in his wilder youth, had been his Deux Chevaux: did one really want a Porsche? The Jesuits might think it funny and just as likely they might not. There are doctors who would giggle and think 'typical Ray' – the present number being a Beetle many years old.

Upon the whole, and with regret, a temptation which had to be resisted. The thing would be stolen within a week. Temptations do get resisted; some do anyhow. Jokes are made about casuistry, about being jesuitical. Dr Valdez is however the real thing, no mummery about that. The Society is and always has been eminent in the sciences and there is nothing in the least extraordinary about Raymond Valdez. Questions remain unanswered: to be a doctor is a help, in being a Jesuit? One dislikes the word 'help'; a coloured, a loaded, almost a partisan word. It might be fair to say 'contributes'. But turn the question round: being a Jesuit quite unambiguously helps towards being a good doctor. Such things aren't in the least unheard-of. Believer and unbeliever frequent the altars of research institutes. Ray might instance Jacques Arnould 'who does space studies', adding rather naughtily 'Of course, he's a Dominican'. Unbelief, disbelief? One can refuse atheism but that's no barrier to being anticlerical.

Part One

People think mostly of the Seine's right bank as the 'grand' side of Paris, because of the Etoile and the vista up the Champs Elysées; the Louvre and expensive shops; pompous squares and immense avenues. Older people have a hazy notion that the left bank means students, and artists y'know, since here is the Sorbonne and what used to be the Latin Quarter. Here though runs – through the sixth and seventh districts – what Proust knew as the Faubourg Saint-Germain: here were the historic town houses of the dukes and princes.

Nobody ever designed better architecture; the happiest mix of formal balance and intimate gaiety: the courtyards are especially delectable. Few now remain undivided, with their original furniture, pictures, panelling. They've been made into Ministries – swallowed by banks, monstrous finance corporations, with bits sublet to the enormously wealthy. There might still be a duke or so hidden away *côté jardin*; and there is a Marquis – with whom William is here concerned. His is one of the oldest names of royal France. Proust-readers remember that they're all related; my cousin-This and my aunt-That: Monsieur le Marquis does this too. It is typical of him that he lives in the historic 'Hôtel' of his ancestors, and that he is extremely rich.

Equally typical are many ramifications and relations in other worlds than that of dukes. Politics for example: he is old now, retired from 'affairs', seldom seen in public. But it is 'remembered' (memory is short in politics) that he has been a Minister of Foreign

Affairs, had a stretch at The Interior. Under an earlier Republic he'd
certainly have been Premier: the Duc de Broglie comes to mind, or
(much better comparison) M. de Talleyrand.

William is not intimidated by these surroundings; they are familiar to him. The concierge, a rude man (his wife is worse and they are
known as *les Cerbères*), looked up and nodded. He crossed the courtyard noticing everything from old habit; the usual cars in their places
and the Rolls too. Nothing changed here; the secretary was where he
expected. Patricia (notable for independence of mind; she even
refuses to eat here), a quiet, compact woman in her forties, smiled,
they'd always got on well.

"Hallo – what brings you here?"

"Hoping for a word with the old man, what are my chances?"

"Good, I should say. He's in the library, be pleased to see you. No
one at present, I should go on up. As well though to clear with Edith,
just to be tactful." Everything here is very Old-France, the boiseries
and the marvellous stucco, the Beauvais upholstery, and furniture
(he had learned) by Oeben, by Weisweiler. Fresh flowers everywhere,
Edith's work. She is the *gouvernante*, rules the household, the companion and betimes the nurse, certainly an ex-mistress (but there's
no evidence). Nobody makes jokes about Mrs Danvers. A strong
personality. Her office is a pretty, sunny morning-room but she isn't
there. He picked up the house phone to call the kitchen.

Charlotte answered, another strong character, insists upon her
Sundays, goes to Mass at Sainte Clotilde, is from La Rochelle and
has an earthy pattern of speech, enjoyed by the Master. Also a glori-
ous cook – he used to eat in the kitchen with her and Léon the chauf-
feur and Jacqueline the Belgian housemaid. She squawked on
hearing his voice.

"Are you back?"

"Just dropped in I'm afraid. Edith's not there?"

"Was, a second ago, I'll tell her if I see her. Come in for a cup of
coffee, before you go." They'd all been a happy family.

He put the phone down feeling the presence: Edith was behind
him. Neither smiling nor glacial; exactly as when she saw him
daily.

"Good morning William. You want to see him? Good, that'll cheer him up – you know the way." She never has been hostile; she knows that fidelity, here, is of long standing, thoroughly tested. He had been, for unusually long, the head of security here, the chief bodyguard. Others came and went but he had grown to be the old man's intimate, and shadow. Between Monsieur le Marquis and himself came to be understanding and affection. Indeed when he left, the old man rang the Minister. 'Don't bother to send me more guards – I don't want any.'

One didn't knock on doors here. He was sitting at the map table.

"William! Agreeable surprise." Always good manners, stands up at once, gives the old affectionate pinch to the forearm.

"Make yourself comfortable. You're looking well. Kind of you to think of passing." In the six-month interval the old man had aged; something of a shock. The temperature was kept low in this house 'because of the furniture' (Patricia is always chilly), really because he hates it hot. Air-conditioning was another grievance. (When in Washington, two sources of complaint.) Now he has a cashmere shawl across the shoulders. Hair cut short, greyer and thinner. The fair-haired sixfooter has shrunk. No more jokes about Visigoths or Gaston Phoebus – 'ancestor of mine'.

Edith brought in the pretty coffee service with the forget-me-nots – he dislikes the Sèvres 'bleu du Roi'.

"Thank you. None for me. But what brings you to Paris? This can't be just for me."

"Joséphine."

"Ah, of course. A mightier inducement." That the Marquis had slept with her was certain. Well known for climbing into bed with every woman he comes across. No pretences are needed, no hints or allusions will ever be made. A thing he does. A thing Joséphine does? William's wife was a complicated woman but this was all ancient history. The old man had never complained at his leaving; getting married was a thing people did. Some very good silver as a wedding present.

"The truth is," said William, "I want your advice".

"Quite right, I give good advice. Nobody takes it, a grave mistake. Think it can't be disinterested. Think it harsh. But sweet words butter no parsnips." Proud of his English, which he speaks well. "Sounds wrong that, somehow. I beg your pardon – you were saying?"

"They tell me I've got a cancer."

"They do? Where?"

"Something internal. They act vague, I suspect deliberately."

"Mm yes. Liver, sweetbread, so good to eat when it's veal; when it's ourselves we prefer not to dwell. Frightened you, mm?"

"Yes." In William's trade they know all about fear, live with it and learn to handle it. This is something else. "At my age."

"Exactly. I know somebody good. Wasn't a great deal he could do for me but he has remarkable talent – name escapes me for the moment. Leave this with me, William. My own small pains, not a great deal to be done bar the pilgrimage to Lourdes, mm, wouldn't the journalists love that. Well, I've had a busy life. But you, my son. . . not going to have this, are we? You may rely upon me." And William knows that to be the truth. "Apropos, have you mentioned this to your wife?"

"Would it interest her?"

"I think my advice would be don't, not just for the present; having to be sorry won't be much use to either of you. It's in your hands but we're going to pull you through this, you know. . . Leave me now, before I get captious and petulant. Look in on Charlotte, that'll make her day. Stay to lunch, come to that. Pooh, what I eat is off a tray." He was already on the phone. "Patricia – I have a little detective work for you." Waving an adieu.

His kindness is genuine. People discount it, saying it's a trap, a ploy, a red herring. They say he's utterly dishonest, through and through. Total bastard. Even if genuine it'll be turned to his advantage. Even if you found the thread you'd never get it untangled. But William, a simple man, knows this complex man better than that.

"Hal-lo," said Charlotte. "Dear boy, as Father says. Drop of white wine? Sit ye down then. Catch Edith? Making the voice ever so small and sweet she were this morning, a little fella got such a bollocking his teeth were loose in's jaw." True, Edith *governs*. 'Not though in My Kitchen'.

"I bet Father was happy," she went on. "But he's not well, at all – you saw? How long do we have, I wonder. What will we do, William, what will we do?"

"Do like him, pay no attention. What happens, happens." It was, he thought, the advice he had just received.

Dr Valdez at 'the office', Institute ponderously named for a dead-and-gone begetter, Doctor Gustave-Adolph Rietschmieder, asks for tea. Silvia, the secretary shared with two more (she isn't fat-gross, she's fat-comfortable) makes good tea. There is also a web-site and much computerized machinery; one can talk to people, across the world but Ray likes to see and speak with faces, bodies, fingers in the room with him.

All over the world the Crab shows up on screens: a great many people observe it, puzzle over it, try to measure it. Major event right now, noticed by all: there's a lot more of it. It is about to tickle half the western world, say the statistics, which is double the figure of a couple of years back. Ray dislikes all these abstractions. It makes points of light on screens, zigs and zags on graph models, forms odd and stangely pretty patterns. To Ray it has a voice to which he listens; a dialogue might result, inconsistent and unexpected and dare one say amusing?

The public, as well as a lot of doctors, would dearly love there to be plain guidelines – preferably pleasant: Eat wholemeal bread. Drink red wine. The Crab laughs at this and so does Ray; they snigger at biochemists and astrologers (friendly though with either). How would he describe himself? A sort of parapsychologist? – after a few glasses of red wine. He's a Dotty; there are many dotties: they have inexplicable successes – he talks to the Crab and sometimes persuades it to go away: credit should go to the Patient. It can pop off and pop back; misbegotten sense of humour, much like God's. There are letters which run together in acronyms, and can signify complex chemical compounds: one (Jesuit slogan) is AMDG. The

Crab understands Latin, needs no telling that Cancer is also to-the-greater-glory-of-God.

Ad majorem – well, upon occasion – *Dei gloriam* is likewise this still youngish man; fair-haired (mud colour), thin, sallow; a slovenly look, poorly finished, with mad pale eyes; a portrait by Otto Dix, foreseeably a favourite painter of his – 'lovely man, *durch Mitleid wissend*'. Here in Strasbourg as elsewhere Jesuits can be found doing anything. They had a big house here before the Revolution (next to the Cathedral, handsome façade now rather dirty, the Lycée Fustel de Coulanges; another local notable). The Observatory was also theirs, and is still here in a peaceful garden with a dome for the telescopes. You wouldn't see much now in the way of stars, the Rhine valley being sorely polluted; they measure earthquakes and the like, while people like Ray have electronic microscopes, and compose dirty limericks for the edification of colleagues in Berkeley or Ann Arbor. The office has links with the University, antique and respectable seat of learning; mostly with the Faculty of Medicine. It's a European city; long humanist tradition. Dürer worked here, and Baldung Grien – two of Otto Dix's major prophets: heaps more saints. As a young scholastic Raymond has been in England, in Poland, Italy. . . now he's here: who knows what the Jesuits get up to?

He likes his research job, is liked there too; the dottiness is appreciated. He doesn't much like lab work. Too much filtered air and the chimaeras bombinating in a vacuum; too much that is shut away from his realities. He has a taste for raw meat, and so has the Crab. Oncology is boring unless ontological. 'No I don't want everybody to live for ever, but I'd like them to make more of what they have. Happiness is more than a sound prostate. No, I don't suppose the results are much better than roulette.' For the Crab keeps a casino where few win, but Ray has his successes.

His phone rang and Silvia's voice said, "I think you'll want this one."

"Doctor Valdez, could you hold just a second? Monsieur le Marquis would like a word if that's convenient." Fascinating old man. Extremely attractive. A failure he hadn't been willing to admit.

They had liked each other. A long life of falsehood, of dishonesty? It was too easy, to put the failure down to that.

"Raymond dear boy, I have something to interest you. A good man, whom I much value as it happens, is in some trouble with these doctors; lives down your way. Of course I've no right to ask personal favours. I think don't you know you'd find him worth the pains." It would never occur to him that I'd tell him no; and if I did he'd find a way of twisting my arm without seeming to.

"I can look into it. Who's been treating him, do you know?"

"Bend you to my will, can I? A man Rupprecht I do believe." Ray suppressed a giggle in his nose, 'the man' being an eminent professor and the old devil certainly aware of it.

"So you'll let Patricia know, will you? I rely upon you. Thank you, I'm as well as you would expect, perhaps a little more. I'll be interested to hear further about this."

And there'll be something behind it. With that old man there always is.

"Silvia can you get me Professor Rupprecht's secretary?. . . Thank you. . . Annie, good morning. Tell me, have you a man Barton on your book? Yes, as in Bordeaux, and probably within the last few months. The Professor's in the theatre is he? With his permission I'd like you to pull that dossier for me."

And now they are in the pub together. A consultation.

"Is this," asked William, "the line in the old Bogart movie, the start of a beautiful friendship?"

"There's another I like even better; Bogart lying on the boat roof and Robinson sneaking out of the cabin. 'I'm coming out now, soldier, I ain't got no gun.'" Pleased with William's guffaw.

"Ray, that's a nice watch. Crocodile and all. Patek Philippe?"

"Present from a grateful patient. I take bribes too."

"Wear it like that, some boy'll rip it right off you."

"I was getting attached to it, too. Worse – I was getting proud of it. You're quite right."

"No, I'm a cop."

"Tell me about this, it interests me. Let's just decide first what we're eating and drinking."

The police are mostly pretty dim. Brutal thugs, a good few. Or corrupt, racist – you name it. Poorly trained too. But if the odd one shows signs of being intelligent and alert as well as having a good physique, a reasonable background, a good school record – and there are some – then you might get fingered for special training and this is intensive, because being a guard to someone like a Minister is a very delicate job. High failure rate. As I know because I was a starred number. I've shadowed the President, and the Premier, and I ended up Chief, for the Marquis, and there I stayed, a number of years, where most get rotated fairly often.

You get very close; there's an intimacy. In a crowd we are several. In a car even, two. But when he's resting – cup of coffee, going over his speech, wash and brush up – you stay with him even for a little walk in the garden, breath of fresh air after dinner – he learns to accept that. You might get a violent reaction of strain or fatigue; lets his hair down, personal, insulting – 'fellow's a bloody fascist'; you never heard it, it was never uttered. He has to have his moments totally unguarded.

"You're always watching for the dotties, they get in anywhere, mostly they've a piece of paper, a petition, an appeal, sometimes they've a fist, or a knife – or a gun."

"You've a gun."

"Carrying, yes of course we are. Rule is, never to use it, even show it unless bloody well forced. Everything based on non-violence. Fellow comes in arms and legs flying, block him, smother him, hold him but never hit him. You're trained, endlessly, in that. Box with one another, judo, defence to any and every sort."

"But you might get shot, knifed, killed even."

"Yes. That's the hard thing. He mustn't be hurt – held for due process of law. But you – you're expendable. Knowing that, you must never hesitate. Look, let me eat this steak in peace."

"Readiness – all times ready."

"You're not going to stop me eating frites. Nor Béarnaise, neither."

"I'm not about to try," said Ray comfortably.

"Nine tenths of it is preparation – prevention – planning. You've gone over every inch in advance, get the unexpected down to the irreducible. That done. . . with a Chief of State you've always a doctor and an ambulance on standby; reanimation unit. Any history say of a heart you've a cardio man. Nice to know; anyone to ressuscitate it's probably yourself, and you'll get the best there is."

"Cheese? Fruit?"

"Sure – I like a lot of both." Ray put his knife and fork together, wiped his mouth, took quite a powerful swig of water.

"Here endeth the first consultation. You've given me the key to what I wanted. A complete non-violence. There are a number of highly aggressive answers to a cancer. Surgery, radio, chemo, any amount of clever little molecules chemists put together and hide inside the pretty pink pill. I don't like any of these much. We've some active things too for me to think about; has to be in tune with you. Active and alert without any violence – did you have lessons in relaxation?"

"Sure: physiotherapist, unwinding. Techniques to do it alone."

"You start that up afresh. I know a girl, good masseuse."

"Does she have a cunt?"

Ray began to giggle but it turned into an outright laugh so that he had to put down his coffee-cup to stop it spilling.

"I haven't looked. You can always try."

"While I've still got a dick and you haven't cut it off."

"William, you better believe me, that'll be the very last thing I'll come to. Don't think of me as castrated – I like girls too."

Ray drove home singing a little song.

> I don't want to roam,
> I'd rather stay at home –
> Living on the earnings of a whore.

Dr Valdez lives in a slice of the old town stuck between two main roads, traversed by a couple of alleyways and disregarded by brisk municipal developers; not old enough to be picturesque with cobblestones, expensive little shops, tourists taking photographs; darkened by high smelly walls whose decrepit plaster is falling off the stonework. These buildings are pinched too close together and the upper stories compete for air and light; sanitation and electricity date from the century previous to the last and are dodgy. But the rents are low. At the street level blank sinister doorways long innocent of paint open on dark tunnels full of dustbins and rusty bicycles, plywood mailboxes with yellowed cards stuck to them. His just says 'Valdez'. You aren't going to say 'Doctor'.

The other advantage is in being perfectly anonymous. Nobody is curious round here. Unsuccessful artists, down-at-heel waiters, old women in bedroom slippers, none of them bothered about Arab neighbours with odd tastes in cookery and music; nobody is racist either – couldn't afford it. On the ground floor junk is stored by dealers in old wood and scrap iron; up the stairs there are queerer, possibly more sinister commodities. Since it is bang in the centre of the city people work round-the-corner, and always underpaid. The police are not unknown, nor debt-collectors. Valdez fits in nicely.

The stairs are stone to the second floor, wood thereafter and children fall down them now and again: there is of course no lift. Walls of dilapidated dark-green paint. The slum-landlord is some insurance company, quite strict about fire hazards. These old buildings don't bring in much but the ground will be valuable some day. Raymond goes up lightly. His view is mostly of gutters, chimney-pots and roofscape but he has quite a lot of space, keeps it more-or-less clean, and is comfortable. His furniture seems mostly to have come from the junkstore downstairs, but people buy the new and the fashionable, throw things away that are perfectly good; the cooker and the hi-fi had cost little.

Ray has taught himself to be a pretty good cook. Also a fervent listener to music. Devotion. Good instincts. Knows, really, damn-all about either subject. Is this jesuitical of him, he wonders? You, and all that you have and do, are His. Jesuits have often been the most deplorable people; appalling reactionaries leagued with the worst sorts of government. One's faith in God's infinite wisdom gets badly shaken here. Mm: your conceit, Valdez, your infernal self-importance – it hasn't been for want of Telling.

You are to think about William. You were a bright little boy but, it was the Society that put you where you are. William is badly blocked, and inside that magnificent physique who knows what fearful knots accumulate – just the thing to attract the Crab.

Autistic children for instance – so little understood, so notoriously difficult to treat – their blockages are such that they roll themselves into a ball in the corner, unable to speak, showing their misery through a sudden frenzy of the most intense violence but they can, with great patience, be brought back into the world – running a thermograph on William might show up places where some of these blockages can be Got At.

This is a tool Dr Valdez thinks quite well of – a sensitive instrument which reads temperatures over fifty strategic points of the bodily surface and gives you a printout on the computer. How very crude – but doctors with fingertip-feel, says Ray sadly, are few and far between. Our pathetic little bits and scraps of Science. Artists have it. Pettish, to still his own blockages. Some music – something jarring which is then most satisfyingly resolved – piano concerto, Ravel, pianist is the Argentine woman. Has she ever got Fingertip-feel. Stay very still and you will feel her hands, on your stomach, searching out and resolving all that is blocked in yourself.

It is not to be. The phone started ringing. One is never invulnerable. The phone shouldn't be ringing; it's an unlisted number. Which in turn means – oh dear. When it rings and one Knows who that is, it's madly welcome, it's extremely unwelcome, but either way, goodbye Monsieur Ravel. Hereafter, in a better world than this, I'll be hoping for more love and knowledge of you.

"Yes." He wants more love and knowledge of Janine, but oh dear. Tears. Snuffles. A pathetic little voice.

"I've been trying to reach you."

"I've been working. I am working. I have again to be working."

"I have to see you."

"I came in to change my shoes."

"But darling, I – " This must be stopped. He wants to say, Darling, tell me your troubles. Better – Come here at once. Now.

"This evening. Come this evening. We'll have a picnic."

"But then I'm at work." Limp with despair.

"Come after work." Knowing he shouldn't say that.

"Is that the best you can do?" Reproach-filled.

"It will be the best. I promise. I must run. Kiss." No kiss. Clonk went the thing, burning with resentment. He wished – he wishes – but there's not much to be had out of that.

Trapped in his own lies – now he has to change his shoes. And make a shopping list. He hadn't been in any hurry to go to work, and now he had to: Janine is quite capable of coming over here to see whether it was true, to catch him.

It's quite a snug cabin. Shelves of books and one or two nice pictures; he hasn't space for more, nor light; there are far too many books. From these surroundings you could fairly conclude that he has money to spend. There is a cupboard with clothes which are well cut and have cost a lot, because Dr Valdez has to go out into the World quite often. The shopping list nags at him so he goes to look in the kitchen, dragging rather. In the fridge is a piece of beef, getting rather sticky too. Well, for tomorrow a paprika stew. He could wish for veal (osso bucco is a lip-smacking idea) but nobody in their senses buys veal now. This will have to do – buy tomatoes. Wants lemon-peel. Wants – no, that we've got; olives we've got, anchovies we've got – or not with lemonpeel? There will be a delicious smell. Janine will provide another delicious smell. Write champagne, write flowers, write something nice-to-put-on-bread: picnic, ja. Rather a long list. Oh well, all in a good cause.

One shoe off and one shoe on Raymond sat paralysed with his mouth open; he has just thought of a good definition of Art. He looks for these a lot because nobody ever knows what Art is, and scientists are thirsty for a bit of it, getting their little particles littler, and perhaps when we find Higgs' Boson it'll turn out to be God. An eighteenth-century English painter-poet wanted a bow of burning gold, and that is unsurpassable? It's a very stiff test; he doesn't know many places where that is to be found. He could say where he first encountered it; on the floor of the Mauritshuis in The Hague, in front of the big Vermeer – do an about-turn and there is the Girl in the Turban. A few more chariots-of-fire he could point to, where you'd expect them, in the world-cities, where civilization has been building up for centuries – the Best we can Do, in gallery or concert-hall.

But how long do the arrows-of-desire take in flight? Five or ten minutes on a stage, and no more for a sunset; he has known pitifully little. The nature of the bow is that it will not resonate for more than the moment or two after Shakespeare ceased to inhabit the actor, Verdi the conductor.

Of these he has caught glimpses now and then. But in bed with a girl? Fellow says somewhere – Never never never never never. That is pretty strong but I am not totally convinced that either in science or in art is there a definitive never. There is so much that I do not understand. There is another man within me, who is angry with me. One of them is in love with Janine. Desire intense, passion over-whelming, let him only think of her he can think of nothing else. Pain. Doctor Valdez knows a lot about pain. Can claim to be an expert on the subject. Every fibre shudders, every nerve twangs hor-ribly, gut and heart and lungs screaming, it's in the throat and in the sinus and reaches down to the finger tip; he can be lying quietly and it will jerk him upright. He gets up and drinks a glass of water and walks about barefooted waiting for it to simmer back down to toler-able level. It's love, this? If a man could go through childbirth it might be like this.

There are lucid intervals, pain of a different nature, is it a sort of withdrawal-symptom, no, that is a cheap and over-facile remark. It is less physiological. The eating and drinking her, the breathing her, absorbing her, that will come again, catching you up and flinging you down. This is less greedy but you love her perhaps the more. You aren't quite as wolfish; are you less famished? Or is this the man within?

We were here and we didn't want to go out. We got very hungry but the idea of phoning for a pizza nauseated both of us, the China-man, the hamburger-man, nonono. Cooking suddenly became funny, we went through the fridge for leftovers, through the shelf for tins, Raymond – that skilful fellow – made wonderful (really they were very good) fishcakes. Three for each. He watched Janine's tech-nique with these, fascinated. She put a great deal of 'mexican' ketchup on all three, scraped it all off to eat with the first, put as much again on the other two and polished that off with the second, repeating this with the last. Ray was delighted. He didn't feel insulted (taken pains to make the things nice). He didn't think her vulgar or greedy. He wasn't disgusted when she used her finger to catch any traces on the plate, licked it and said she wished there were more. If he had thought about it at all he would have said it showed trust; that she felt confidence, was comfortable with him, able to let her hair down. It was loveable in her.

He couldn't, probably, have described her, even physically. That would not have thrown doubt upon his truthfulness, accuracy, nor detachment. He loved her. One would have to have asked William – quite a while later. His accuracy of observation struck everyone, including Ray. Trained cop, trained and experienced bodyguard: normal.

"Janine? I only met her once, no, twice. I had dinner with them in a restaurant. Ray brought her to show off. Her table-manners were perfect, altogether the lady. She was an actress, not very good; highly professional though. Very attractive, tremendous magnetism. Wonderful dancer, marvellous legs. Well – durably – put together. Marvellous tits too.

"Not beautiful but pretty, fine features. The only thing bad, small narrow eyes. Blue, a sharp electric blue, bit of green in it. Made up well. Lovely nose and ears, wide mouth well cut. Wide high cheekbones, not really Slav, fine forehead. Fair hair; she would have tanned well. Good deep voice, quite a lot of range. Handled herself well. Skilled. Anyhow some talent, I never saw her on a stage.

"She picked up bit parts pretty often, enough for a living. Ray told me she'd failed for the Conservatoire here, 'in a year of lots of good girls'. Don't know if that's true, she was an accomplished liar. Tried out for television here, they didn't want her. Had a go in Paris, got a few film parts. Knew her trade, could have made her way no doubt. But expensive flat, sharp little sporty car, spent a lot on clothes, so always broke.

"No, she wasn't on the tap, not with Ray anyhow. Little sums maybe, he bought her things but no jewellery or stuff – keepsakes. It would be a big mistake to think of her as grabbing or even false. A generous streak and a lot that was genuine. Of course, I can only go by what he told me. I think she made up stories, didn't know herself whether they were true or false; all muddled together as I'd guess, in her mind. But when it came to trouble I wasn't surprised."

One would give a lot of weight to William's view of people seldom met and scarcely known. Among others 'M. le Marquis' confirmed that; said William was unusually shrewd at summing up a character and that he'd often found it so. Pretty shrewd himself as well as crooked; probably a good witness. Especially as to whores. Back for a moment to William –

"No I don't think you'd call Janine a whore. Came awfully close perhaps, now and then. She was quite intelligent. On the whole, possibly, she was too damn complicated." Ray himself said that she was given to 'acting out her own fantasies'.

"You don't understand her" warm in her defence. "So very vulnerable, so sensitive, so little confidence in herself. A broken family, nobody to care for her, she's had some hard times." It is fairest no doubt to all concerned to leave it at that.

Doctor Valdez has no 'consulting room'. He has his being in the office at the Institute, where his mail goes, and he keeps his papers. Here now he sits, and he's thinking that 'this won't do'.

This so far is nothing but bits and scraps; jerky, jagged fragments of life. Now he must put it together, smooth it out, and make a plan.

I was called into consultation quite a time ago, to go to Paris, take a look at Monsieur le Marquis. This suggestion did not come from eminent colleagues in Paris who were already treating him. That could happen, does occasionally, but hadn't. Which makes for difficulties. Deontology: one will not criticize nor interfere with treatment prescribed by eminent colleagues who haven't asked my opinion. It came from the Marquis himself, who had heard of me God-knows-where and wasn't saying. He was very insistent that I should have a shot. He has of course the right to consult whom he pleases, including charlatans. I was not in a happy position but did not see my way to refusing.

I didn't get far with this. Clinically the crab had got too much of a grip on him. He had refused surgery. The eminent whosis had put him on a good standard treatment which would keep him going quite a while yet. I made efforts to get inside this man, and the best I could do was to get alongside. We liked each other, had some good talk about this-and-that. It stopped short of any real understanding. A politician in all his fibres, hardened and polished by the years; intensely secretive, incredibly devious, and one has to say it, fundamentally dishonest. I had to say what I had been in little doubt of from the start.

"I can't treat you." No foothold, but this old man neither needs nor wants explanations, metaphors, illustrations. He has courage, an immensely sharp intelligence, a remarkable lucidity.

"You need not worry about it, Raymond. Most men are tools; they come to my hand, I use them. You are not a tool. I enjoy knowing you. You increase my self-knowledge. That is a gain I do not think lightly of. There are those who prolong my life and I am grateful. Others – yourself – I gain in profundity."

"I don't much like this profit and loss talk." The old man has a delightful smile. No doubt it has often served him well but that does not interest me.

Six months later I get a call from him, asking me to look at William. Of course I accept – I owe him that much. I don't even have to go to Paris; William lives in my back yard.

Very likely I shall have to go to Paris. This wife – Joséphine – separated, not divorced, is a key, no doubt of it. If I am to do serious work here I must try to know something of this woman.

Clinically speaking – I have seen the dossier, and Rupprecht's notes: I have talked to him. I have a chance here. Rupprecht's policy is mostly defensive. He doesn't think there is much he can do beyond a skilful delaying action. I am not so sure. For the crab to step backwards is not unknown. To abandon altogether – not unheard of. That depends upon the subject. I call William a pretty good subject.

It begins to be sure with this firm principle, the refusal of violence. There at our first meeting, in that country restaurant, he had a good and well-told tale.

"Violencia. . . Once, a while back, this wasn't Marky but old Lavigne when he was President, I was drafted for state visits in

South America. The Ol' Man was mad on Incas or whatever, there we were, Olmecking & Toltecking. One temple, we were lodged in a tourist place, I was on duty, little man walks in asking for the Boss. He had a little cardboard suitcase – I want that open, it was full of rocks. What d'you want? Sell you this for five thousand dollars. A fortune to him. Says it's raw emeralds. I can't do that. And isn't it dangerous? I can protect myself, he says, and shows me this gun he has, old seven-sixty-five Mat, wouldn't shoot a paper doll. Cheap, cheap, he kept saying, me with my three words of Spanish. Three men walked in at the door just like a Western movie, without a word they put three shots in him right in the hotel lobby, behind the desk there's a clerk and a guard, local man. I'm behind the sofa smartish, they blew all three to pieces, goddam great Colt forty-five, I've never seen so much blood. I don't know what Lavigne got beyond a lot of official apologies, I got a pair of emerald ear-rings, Joséphine has them." Wonderfully Bald. I have plenty to learn, here.

"So no belief in violence, personal or professional."

"Sounds odd from a cop, all right."

"The girl who was raped by the anaesthetist, only her word for it, entire clinic ganged up to say impossible, her fantasy, no proof whatsoever, what would you advise her?"

"Get a little cutter, held in the palm, do him across both cheeks, it's old-fashioned but mighty efficient."

"But since you're an old pirate you'd tip him the black spot first, wouldn't you? Let him sweat."

"You're quite right, it solves nothing. Childish. She can call him up and breathe at him. Fear."

"Will it hit his conscience?"

"He hasn't any. Miserable bugger."

"Your logic's good. You can only get him through the colleagues but protecting him they protect themselves. Even when they know it's true, fear for their job, reputation, money."

"But they'll see to get rid of him quietly, and he won't get another job."

"Does that help the girl who got raped?"

"Plenty girls get raped, learn to live with it."

"Less bad."

"She's got to begin somewhere. Who raped me? – poor feeble type – I'll paddle my own canoe, not worry about his."

"Much better."

"Place is full of crooked cops," remarked William indifferently.

"What d'you do about them?"

"Nothing. Make up your own mind – you're going to be straight or you're going to be bent. Individual choice. Guard work, that's different. Knew we depended one on all the others. Weak sister there, we threw him out. No choice."

Ray remembers – and it's no coincidence – his conversations with the Marquis. Exactly this same point, of the difference between a collective responsibility and the individual.

They were in the library. The old man liked to talk with, through or around books. A lovely room, on the shaded side and the light filtered, to protect these beautiful bindings.

"Fine bindings – pooh. Oh there's good stuff here but most of mine are upstairs. Here in France we just put on a paper cover. Liked the old days myself; had to cut the pages, some effort involved, knew you'd read the book, then."

"But these are beautiful," said Ray amused.

"Yes indeed. And some are good. But the English – why do they bother? Good sturdy hardwearing cloth, dustjacket, lot of effort and thought gone into that. Even when it's trash inside. . . The world is a very evil place" suddenly.

"So we say, in the Company."

"Books have taught me much, that we don't learn in the diplomatic service. Politics, bah." He got up, walked across, opened a bookcase. "You never read *Lord Jim*?"

"No." Ray thinks he 'might have heard of it'.

"A case in point," said the Marquis, rather in the manner of a minister handling a question in the National Assembly. "Asks this same – interesting – moral question." Turning the book in his hands as though about to guess its weight, talking to it. "Old-fashioned romanticism." That might have been a dire disease endemic in tropical climates. "Concerns a young officer in the Merchant Marine – a corporation with severe standards. Idealist young man." (Blackwater fever, thought Ray; decidedly not a thing to catch.) "Looks forward to a supreme test of courage in emergency. Fails it. Not altogether his fault, he's got involved in a crooked deal. Jumps overboard from a sinking ship – only it doesn't sink. At the subsequent inquiry, is given a severe blame, loses his ticket, with it his job. Black disgrace." It must have been this that Ray would recollect months afterwards in the pub with William, thinking of the doctor's fatal calamity. Struck off the register. . .

"Mm, it rather falls to pieces from there on. Kindly old man gives him a second chance to make good, as agent for trading company, tropical jungle, island somewhere in Dutch Insulinde. Natives think him a hell of a chap, upright you know, justice, truth. Arrives a melodrama, the details I spare you – can't remember them myself – involves his word given, to which he must be faithful. Local chieftain convinced of treachery – shoots him. Dies knowing he has kept his word when he could have saved himself. Mourned by all – greatly respected. Much good did it do him. I haven't in the least given you a sympathetic picture" putting the book back in its place lovingly. "I used to collect for fine examples of the binder's art, for illustrations by a good painter. Decorative, often really beautiful. Tendency to neglect or forget the text inside. A real book you keep in your pocket, not wrapped up in cotton wool. Look, I've three editions here of Shakespeare. Upstairs is the one I read – lower deck for the use of." There were more moments of this kind, for books, Dr Valdez thought, were the royal road to this complicated old man. With a book he was no longer devious, would not be crooked. If only I'd got here earlier, thought Ray, sadly.

He was thinking now of that scrumptious house up on the hillside where William lived. Had he seen any books? He'd only been in the one room . . .

"What d'you like to read?"

"Never read any books at all." That is one answer. Another, more to be despised, comes from people ashamed of being thought illiterate. "Never seem to get the time for reading now." But really it had been an idle question. That was not the road to William.

"Don't tell me you look at the television."

"Christ no."

"So what d'you do? Toy trains? Model ships? Or just sharpen your knives?"

"Pretty good question. I used to – professional skills, gym, judo, box a bit. Tell the truth – faggoty it sounds – I used to do uh, modern dance group. Too tall though, too heavy. Still, liked that. Hell of a discipline, everything else leaves your mind. I'd like now. . . teach myself wood carving." (Teach myself, notice, as against go-and-learn; does the choice of words point to anything?). "No – plain carpentry. Make – make – desk with drawers. That's very difficult. Make table, to stand even on four legs, that's already a tall order."

"It's just you and no one else?"

"That I agree is the weak point." Is it possible that the thought of Janine stopped Raymond from asking further?

"Books have been my faithful friends."

"Too damn rarefied for me. Or too goddam stupid. Who's going to waste time asking who killed Roger Ackroyd?"

"Millions have."

"Can't any of them be policemen."

"People like to be mystified. Look at the last page myself, first. There are other sorts of book," mildly.

"I've seen them, too. Want to make my flesh creep," with a massive contempt. "Psycho fellow, knife, lies in wait for little children. I've spent too many years with the real thing."

"The world is very evil," thinking of the Marquis.

"Yes it is. I've seen some things, Ray. Before I got tapped to rub along with the Great – a few psycho types there, I could tell you some stories – I was PJ. On the street, on the beat. Police reporter comes, get his story for the paper. Wants a bit of blood to tickle up the readership. Know what he always leaves out, what he wouldn't thank us to give him? The smell, mate, the stink. You won't find that, in any of the books."

"William please do forgive me, I hate to say this, I have in fact worked the night shift on the casualty station in the Hotel Dieu – the well-named – I know what the police brings in and what the cat drags in, the thirty-six-hour-duty on the minimum legal wage and I know I don't look it but I've fished the broken glass out of arseholes too, I know what it's like, the bedside manner was an afterthought, Jesuits are also Police Judiciaire and are told off to shovel shit."

"I'm sorry, I was being dim."

"Everybody thinks his is the only cancer, it's perfectly normal."

I wonder whether I might not have a shot at turning William into a Janeite. That sounds absurd; a Frenchman of his background and position. Never mind: circumstances, situations call for eccentricities of thought as well as of physical treatment. In many ways I want to loosen him. I think of acupuncture, and of a method familiar in Germany: a system of small injections at chosen points in the body's surface (the thermograph will give me indications) or quite small shots of an ordinary local anaesthetic, which have a well-known effect in freeing and shortcutting hidden blockages. But there has to be more. The 'Humberstall-Effect'; brilliantly described by an English writer. (I don't know who reads Kipling nowadays: I do.)

I introduced the Marquis to this – to this day it is "my invention". He was delighted. Of course he loves English literature, is familiar with a great deal, though he didn't know this. In the past, he said, he had "tried Jane", but missed the point, was amused by the rediscovery. We came – for we value laughter, a powerful aid to any therapy – to use the slogan when we met.

"Believe me, there's no one like Jane in a tight place." It is probable that William will know little or nothing of the background. The Marquis, a much older man, highly sophisticated and well read, has a strong sense of history, and caught on very quickly. People in general know something of the second world war but have fogotten what they ever knew of the first. The '14–18. People no longer understand how much this meant, how deep it went. So I'm going back to the start of this story, since William is going to need that.

Humberstall – a humble man – is a simple soldier with an artillery unit; a good soldier, immensely strong and a bit thick. He gets invalided home after being blown up by shellfire. In the hospital nobody can find much wrong with him; what would come to be called shell-shock was then little understood, but his none-too-bright wits are further dazed. He makes his own way back to his comrades out of instinct. His commander, a kindly man, has no use for him but finds a neat solution: "I particularly want you as a mess waiter." He can hang about polishing things, perfectly happy.

The unit's guns are old-fashioned things on rails, largely worn out and 'not much use this late in the war': they have a quiet position well behind the front lines, forgotten by authority.

This story would be no more than an anecdote without a peculiar psychological fact. The three officers have suffered the intense strains of their service, have seen their guns shunted aside as worthless, and have lost interest in the hostilities. To someone like myself, there is a parallel with a patient of William's sort. They are cynical, since they serve no real purpose, but should the Germans bombard them they are in danger of death or mutilation. Their escape from this combination of risk and boredom is to play a typically English literary game with the characters of Jane Austen: the world where 'nothing ever happens'.

The Marquis was wonderfully quick at picking up constructions. "Of course," he said at once. "I suppose the only really major novelist in any language whose world has totally banished war, violence, death and mutilation – or cancer come to that. The English are all mad on her – it's worse than Trollope."

The officers have the solidarity between themselves of belonging to a 'secret society'; they are the Janeites. Only one other man shares in this, a soldier with education, a sly and even sinister man, exactly the type who wangles himself a good job in prison. He is of course the officers' mess orderly, simply because he too knows how to talk about Jane.

Poor Humberstall can make nothing of it: what are they all on about? The crafty one offers, for payment naturally, to introduce him to this secret world, and night after night he has to read the books, wondering what they, too, are all about! But this as promised pays off; he gets tips, and is indeed treated as privileged, exempt from all tedious military chores. No wonder that he is very happy. "Our little group, there was no one to touch us."

This idyllic life cannot last, and does not. The German attack of March 1918 swamps their safely forgotten position. They are bombarded, the unit is destroyed, the others are all killed, and Humberstall, intact and bewildered, finds himself 'the only Janeite left'. But even in the mess and confusion of evacuation he remembers his passwords, quotes Jane to a hospital sister and is rewarded by a safe passage out. "I expect she was the Lady Catherine of the area," he says, delighted. Years after, finding himself looked after and kindly treated, he will put his good fortune down to being a true Janeite. As he tells Kipling, "I reread all her books still for pleasure, and then I remember it – right down to the smell of the gluepaint on the screens."

The Marquis was enchanted – "I see it all". He must indeed have known and frequented many a chalky old general who had been a junior officer in the trenches of '14. "Do you think there would be any female Janeites?"

"There was the sister, to whom he said 'Stop Miss Bates there talking' – but in general I should think it's a man's world. And very English."

"One can't be sure. Kipling loved France, and has always been popular here."

To enrol William as a Janeite is tempting; it's a possible means of approach. I would want to know rather more about him, and in particular about his wife. Whom I must meet, and this is to be arranged.

I can hear a lot of people – not all of them French – clicking their tongue and tutting at my frivolity. Here is a doctor, with qualifications in neuropsychiatry and quite some experience in the field, amusing himself with jokes of this sort. It would be easy to knock such people on the head with professional jargon; there's plenty of that about. To tell the truth I haven't a lot of patience with them. The French are world-champion swallowers of anti-depressant pills, cherish them as a child its teddybear. Very well, to restore sanity adopt simple language.

It is logical to be depressed if suffering from a grave malady. Melancholy affects William. The classical pointers to depression are easily described: irritability; a diminished interest in most normal spheres of activity; loss of weight; tendency to insomnia, fatigue and loss of energy; devaluation of the professional role (the feeling of being useless and guilt about that); a weakened ability at organizing one's own existence; recurrent gloomy thoughts about death – it could be with an urge towards suicide; inaptitude at ordinary social obligations.

It gets said at school that any five of these adds up to a syndrome. In consequence nine-tenths of the population describes itself as depressive; I do so myself. Congratulating themselves upon the important discovery they rush to their family doctor demanding the fashionable pill: since, alas, doctors are judged by the number and variety of their prescriptions (it's an over-crowded profession), all too often they get it. William, robust as he is, hasn't thought of this yet. But it's quite likely that he will.

I could get pretty technical about all this. In fatally loose talk about depressions (the media are full of it) one is describing an illness and neglecting the patient. The clinician, general or psychiatric, is caught between his job of prescribing and that of studying how the patient puts himself together. Question of experience. It's a happy-pill, a feel-good, and on the same level really as any of the ecstasy drugs? Not really; they aren't in the strict sense habit forming and can be in the long run a necessity, almost like insulin to a diabetic.

The experienced doctor throws a bit of cold water on these people's tendency to enjoy their own ailments. 'Certainly it's a depression, but it's a very Mild one isn't it. Now that you understand it you can perfectly well take it in hand.'

Ever since Dürer described Melancholia all artists do this, really. Kipling suffered a good deal from depression; wrote about it often. That is the artist's way of exorcizing it. But if you are no artist, to become a Janeite is pretty good therapy.

We pass it on, you know, by whatever means.

When it comes to the point Dr Valdez doesn't want at all to be rid of his beautiful watch; turns it over in his hands, revelling in it. Jesuits

are not encouraged to material attachments. In fact the words of
Saint Teresa come to mind, as cited by one of his early professors.
A new young novice asked permission to keep a pretty prayerbook,
given her in childhood, of which she was very fond. 'Fond of it, are
you?' said that formidable lady. 'Better not come in here then.'

Are their names not sweet symphonies?

Lines by Dante? A sonnet by Petrarch?

'Audemars-Piguet, Vacheron-Constantin,
Girard-Perregaux, and Jaeger le Coultre,
Piaget, and Langen-und-Söhne,
Breguet
And Patek Philippe.'

No: he refuses. Be ashamed about that, will he? Have to come to a
decision? Well, he'll think about that tomorrow.

Monsieur le Marquis had a funny story. In a moment – they are
volatile – of probably drunken euphoria he had bought himself a
Rolex; worn it for a few days 'getting steadily more uneasy'. In a
moment – yes, another – of extreme exasperation he had thrown it
on the bathroom floor where it exploded, shattering into satisfying
fragments. In the French declamatory-rhetorical mode, as when
addressing the National Assembly –

'Oyster – return to your native waters – by way of the plug hole.'
With that suppressed laugh from somewhere high in his sinus.
'Vulgar thing.'

A jeweller, for Jesuits are like jackdaws and collect anything that
glitters, had told him that stainless steel – 'the 316 L which is used
for the best surgical instruments' – is the thing to have. 'Gold' mag-
nificently 'always looks cheap'. And for a fine movement steel gives
the best protection. Ray had wondered, ever so little, whether he
wasn't getting led up the garden path.

'It was Patek Philippe who first set steel with diamonds.'

'Mine has no diamonds.'

'On that very account,' said the old man charmingly, 'yours is the
best there is. It is with the greatest simplicity that one reaches the
greatest elegance.'

'What about those people with ice on their beards, in the *National Geographic*?'

'It pays to advertise.'

Raymond put his watch back on. Buckled the strap. Keeping.

Evening; dusk. Alleyway, a few steps from home. No one, then someone, looming. A colossal shock. An extreme, excruciating pain. Blindness. Vertigo. He was on the deck, on his knees. His hands trying to keep his face off the street. Face? Or what is left of it. Vomit? Do, by all means; be my guest. Retch, mostly. After a long time, perhaps a minute or two of pain unspeakable, pulled himself up. Didn't stay up; sat or rolled on to a step. Keep that way, head between your knees. Heard footsteps, fast, then slow, then fast again. A drunk, inna gutter, better not interfere. A while later, Raymond got up, could walk; just about. End of alleyway are bright lights, main road, people. Don't want people, want reason. Want help, want first-aid. Can't see anything much; shadows, lights in streaks. Pharmacy, that's it. Need kind people but need professionals, that's instinct. But also reason. Doorway: stop and have a little rest.

This is the centre of the town. Pharmacy-aplenty. Medieval town, they have medieval names. "Serpent," said Raymond out loud. "Virgin. Rose. Iron Man." Mentally, something was still functioning. Somebody took his arm.

"Man – you need help."

"Yes. Pharmacy."

"Right. Yes. Good idea. Along here. Not far. Can you walk?"

Bright light. Very bright, far too bright. In streaks, a young woman's face, a white overall. She opened her mouth and said "Woo." She took hold of him by the shoulders. "Sit. Here. I'll get the *chef*." Lights zigged and zagged all over the shop. Better with the eyes shut. As long as there are still eyes. Then a man's voice. "That's a nasty smash. Here, drink this."

Admirable; familiar; old-fashioned restorative; just the goddam bloody ticket. Mind – thank heaven – supplies old-fashioned Latin name. Sal Volatile. "Hear me all right can you? We've called the Samu. Be here in just a tick." *Service-ambulance-medicale-*

urgence, oh that's very good indeed. Siren, blue light, winking, professionals.

"Don't need stretcher. I can walk."

"Keep quiet, don't talk," said the voice of authority. "We'll take a quick look." They always do. Heart, chest, spine, pelvis.

"What hit him – a bus?"

"Only facial," said Raymond. "Rest's all right."

"Facial's the word. Lot of pain? Give you a quick shot for that. Chest and limbs are okay. You'll be fine."

"Not as wide as a church door but it'll serve."

"Bit woozy. All right, get him in the wagon and clean him up a bit. Breathe deeply, relax totally, we're taking you in. Any eye-witnesses?"

"No," said Raymond. "Fella mugged me in the alley."

"Charming. Okay then, *ein-zwei-drei*." Experts slid him into the wagon, smooth as the bearers at the funeral.

"Your mouth's fine and so are your teeth," said the girl's voice. "So here's a little oxygen, help pep you up. Next stop Traumatology Centre, you'll need a few repairs."

The duty nurse didn't even say woo; called the intern.

"Who hit you then, mate? – King Kong?" He felt too tired to talk. "Not a great deal I can do right here. Make you more comfortable. We'll have to hold on to you. Radios, see in the morning what the Professor says." They undressed him, must have gone through his pockets because the boy came back. "Doctor Valdez," a bit hangdog. "Just a word." Clearing his throat. "I'm sorry to have seemed abrupt. We'll want some surgery. Make you as good as new. Don't worry about a thing. Important now to have a good sleep." Yes. Nice, the kindly morphia. Dark. Oblivion.

A grey morning, a quiet room, an angel. She really was; she had 'Angèle' on her little plastic nameplate. Comfortable, matter-of-fact and as nurses go she had light kind fingers.

"Going to prep you because the Professor wants you downstairs as soon as may be. Rinse your mouth shall I? I'm going to shave you. The Police want a word – I've told them to eff off. The anaesthetist too if you can bear it, but she's rather a sweetie." A little smiling dark woman. Extraordinary things they do have on their check list; Raymond's private life reviewed in nosy detail but a readiness to enjoy jokes. Everybody very polite. Confraternity conveys privileges, Doctor Valdez. He was in a private room, and his angel at beck and call. Going to be the Man in the Iron Mask for a day or two; give him time to think. For instance he didn't have to look at the Police, who were apologetic but persistent.

"Not just an ordinary mugging, you see. Vengeance like, they wanted to smash you. We've had a word with the Professor; he's explained the radios. Something quite narrow but heavy metal. Like you know knuckleduster. Professional, like. Break your nose but really putting the boot in, like. You never saw? Total surprise? Knew where to find you. Proper ambush. Now what or who could be behind that, would you say?" They would have a lot of trouble believing Raymond's saying that he simply didn't know.

"Can't help us at all? Pity, that. Materially, not a great deal to go on. Uh, Doctor, when you're up and about, you'd have no objection to popping in to the office like, the *Chef* would want to have a word, d'you know?" Only too obvious that they didn't believe a word he said.

When he could see – two beautiful black eyes like that beast, a lemur is it? (all he needed was rings on his tail) – the angel was a great comfort. You couldn't call her Pretty; the sort of ratty dark-blonde hair which looks dirty even when clean – and she was clean from hair to toenails to underpants – and a coarseness of feature, but never mind, she was kind and good, and she got prettier by the day. On the other shifts, nice girls all. Not up to his Angel though.

The Professor dropped in for a chat with Dear-Colleague; alarmingly technical but kindly. Baldish when seen, with bits of fair gingery hair sort of strewn about; more to the point a marvellous pair of hands. The nose – no, his own – might look a bit aquiline, the cheekbones a bit slav, but good-as-new. The antrums and septum and suchlike dodgy affairs had not been as damaged as might have been feared. You've a good hard head, dear colleague; going to be right-as-rain. Consolidating nicely. Don't worry about the headaches; they'll wear off.

Being short on next-of-kin means there aren't any bloody visitors (the police left behind an odd mentholated smell). On behalf of the Company Paul dropped in. He doesn't know Paul at all well; quietish chap, with interests in medieval philosophers, Giordano Bruno and the like, and Paul is not particularly interested in Dr Valdez.

"Anything you want? Clean pyjamas or whatever?" He has always mumbled; his lips move in a funny way. "Books or anything?"

"I'm fine. Lovely girl here got me a toothbrush." Hospitals are accustomed to the living-alone, unperturbed by the homeless, the indigent, or the mad. Angèle had asked whether there were phone-calls needing to be made. Sensible-Silvia (who had just cleared the police off the doorstep) was professionally discreet; cancelled his appointments for the coming days; said nothing to anybody. Janine, subduing hysteria and filled with a humble domestic zeal, was spring-cleaning the flat, in a virtuous glow at getting herself filthy. Paul, being a historian, could never be surprised by anything that might happen. Thus, the Jews of medieval Strasbourg, whose notions of medicine were in advance of beliefs commonly held, had gone outside the town in the search for purer water. But they hadn't reckoned with the accusation of poisoning all the Christian wells, and got massacred in particular nasty fashion. 'Anything that can go wrong will' is also a Jesuit tenet.

It is very good to feel grateful for a network of solidarity. There you were; big-chief Hawkeye. But of a sudden – lost, in the middle of a desert. But you've got your modern-day convenience – your mobile phone, your credit cards, your little briefcase with the magic microchips. Except that you haven't: nightmare. How are you to be rescued? The helicopter appears. It's a big Deputy with a belly and expensive sunglasses, who bawls at you. 'What the hell are you doing here? This is a forbidden area; this whole desert is radioactive; stand here over five minutes you've lost your balls. Papers! No papers? I'm putting handcuffs on you boy. Do your explaining to the Sheriff in Las Vegas; feel grateful if he doesn't slam you in the drunk tank.'

Shuddering Raymond opened his eyes, and there was Paul, placidly smoking a cigar and using a coffee-cup as an ashtray. Mate, if Angèle comes in here she'll have your balls.

"Needed, Paul, is a good Act of Contrition, is what we need."

Because of course Angèle did come in, and made a tirade, about Grown Men, being Fucking Irresponsible. Not, to be sure, the first time the Society has been expelled from the kingdom. Viper in the bosom of Marianne, or a Russian spy in Nevada, you'll get it in the neck. Well – sighing deeply and being very original – God moves in imponderable fashion. Why should anyone take the pains to break the bridge of his nose, in such an unpleasantly precise and spiteful fashion. What is the message? It sounds like 'Boy, straighten up or something worse will happen.' Who is it addressed to? A doctor, a Jesuit, a Russian spy? Is it Do something? Or Stop doing something? On the whole it would be nicer to know.

The day of his discharge he took a look in the glass. Feels still like it's going to be Elephant Man with a trunk or something. And of course it's perfectly normal. Perhaps just a touch more aquiline, but that's a Sign of Distinction. Very good piece of cosmetic surgery.

"Smashing," agreed his angel, in not, perhaps, the happiest choice of phrase. "The slight werewolf look is terrifically sexy." He went out and bought her expensive chocolates.

As soon as Doctor Valdez (Silvia, to be honest) had got his affair in order he drove out to see William, to whom he had sent no message. It was anyhow a fine sunny morning.

The house seemed empty; no answer to his ring: garage door down, couldn't tell whether the Porsche was there asleep. Around the side the garden wall was too high to see over without a ladder. Hm, French privacy. All that work (and a great deal of money) to build a fortress, and 'what for?' There was a door in this wall. Bolted. Looking down to the corner, vines came right up to the level of the garden William had done nothing with, but there was a path, and in the centre of the lower wall a grille, but one would still see nothing, even without the sun in his eyes; the architect had planned that you shouldn't. Terraces had been built to the exact edge of the sightline and the house itself invisible from here. Cunning; one would admire if it wasn't all such a waste.

Oh well, he'd try again before giving up. There must have been a camera in the front porch because William's voice said, "Oh it's you," and the door opened at once. William met him in the hall. He had a gun in his hand. Unnecessary melodrama I'm making there: it was a small rifle, tucked in the crook of his arm.

"Sight for sore eyes. I thought you'd lost interest."

"No. I was unavoidably detained. To make the story short I was in hospital." William put the gun down. "Make the story long."

"I had an accident," said Raymond apologetically. "My nose got broken. I was out of action while they put it together again."

"There is now you mention it something funny about your eyes." Ho: the werewolf look.

"Some bones got remodelled."

"Then that was some broken nose."

"Somebody broke it for me." He didn't know why he said this. Was it because – an idea ridiculously remote – the attack had some obscure link to the man he was talking to? The life of a security guard could include people with exotic tastes. Now William looked at him with a sharp focus, an intensity.

"Come on out to the terrace. Nice morning. I want to hear more about this," picking up his gun.

"What you doing with that?"

"It's a Walther twenty-two. Pretty good with quality ammo." Strolling out to the corner. "How far would you make it to the bottom wall there?"

"Hard to say, with the slope. Fifty surely?"

"Nearer a hundred. Easy for me since I knew already. See the crow?" He threw up the rifle, sighted, there was a dry hard slap, the bird fell off the wall.

"As though shot," faking surprise.

"You try. Backsight's at seventy-five, allow a scrap for wind from left to right."

"No, I'm a Janeite, violence in any form. You shouldn't shoot birds."

"Songbirds I wouldn't. Not many left around here, the local people shoot them, eat the grapes they say. Swarms of cats too. Shoot them if I catch them. I'm violent of a sudden? No, I'm a countryman. And an ex-cop. So now I want to hear what happened to you."

Raymond told the story, bald. Not laughing, the audience; no, but smiling broadly.

"You think this had something to do with me?" Shrewd – and unexpected.

"I can't for the life of me bring it home to anything."

"Then we'll have to find out." Abrupt. "Coffee? No. Drink?"

"Yes, if it's long and pretty unalcoholic."

"Sit," handing him the gun. "S'all right, there's nothing in the magazine. Harmless as a stick," walking off.

This top terrace was flagged. You could shade it when the sun got too hot. There was rattan garden furniture. The terraces below stretched out abandoned, weed-grown; and what a pity. The sunny wall would be perfect for espaliered fruit.

"Lots of lovely things planned," thought Raymond aloud, "and never carried out."

"Just so," coming back with the drinks, "but one thing at a time."

What a fine thing is youth! This was straight back to his time as a student in Cracow. Well, you'd expect Poland to be full of Jesuits, wouldn't you. 'Apple-pie' is the student drink. The Szarlotka is two-thirds cold apple juice and the rest is buffalo-grass vodka: even then he'd been better at medicine than he was at theology. But 'can't remember the name'.

"Zubrówka," said William, pleased.

"These vines yours too?"

"Mr Baron Geoffrey de Sainte-Anne, who lives in the château over there, made a deal with his sister, with rather bad grace, to let her have this corner. Wedding present for me, that was supposed to be. Since the Baron is also the local mayor, and on excellent terms with every local authority, I was looking forward to a life of leisure and a rosy future. I've neither. It seemed a bit rough when I heard about that, but as an ex-cop I don't believe in justice much. Thought I was stepping into a pretty grand world when I married Joséphine. Marky giggled a good deal about that. For him of course these local notables were so many jokes. I go on getting wine from Geoffrey.

He's not a bad chap; bit of an old woman. Tight-fisted crowd, viewed as a whole – nothing stingier than the upper classes."

"Tell me about your own family."

"That's quickly done because there's none of it left. My father was still quite young when he caught his hand in a machine. Septicaemia. My mother, not very long after, had the windows tight shut on a cold winter's night. Carbon monoxide. My brother and myself, big strong boys, thought of serving the Fatherland. Army, and police. He got into a little local difficulty out in Africa, got a posthumous medal for his pains. On the whole – you might say – we seem to have been an unlucky crowd."

"Perhaps," said Raymond, "we'll reverse this string of fatalities. I begin to see it better; you saw your luck turning good. Only then it didn't."

"They've rather an elegant pad in Paris," as though talking to himself. "We lived there while this place was building; I was still with the Marquis. Only one fine day I found I wasn't married any more; it had all been a mistake. I'd do quite well I suppose out of a divorce settlement; she's generous, you know. I haven't done anything about it – and then when I got ill. . . One could sell all this – get rid of that pissy Porsche. Only I keep wondering, what's the point."

William would be a candidate all right, for the select company of Janeites.

"Things are following me round," he went on. "You turn up, and what's more it's Marky who sends you. It's like these damn stupid books – mystery, suspense, call them all sorts of names. Queer things happening. You come here – and somebody mugs you in the alley. I wonder whether I can find out more about that. Sort of job I know how to do. I'd be interested."

"And you're short of things to interest you. You might not be wrong. All right, I've got this chore in Paris, and when I get back we'll be in touch, talk a bit more about matters. . . It's a pity about this garden."

"Yes," said William 'making an aphorism', "never raining when you want it and always when you don't."

William Barton.

People live in little compartments. In the words of the old joke – *les Vicomtes se rencontrent, ils se racontent des histoires de Vicomte*. I've seen a good deal of this.

People who live in a world of privilege, meaning power, wealth, influence, they lose touch with reality.

We were there to protect power. Sort of an in-joke among us. There were those who knew they were vulnerable, depended on us. And those who wanted to pretend we weren't there. Got highly irritable. But mostly they came round, started to understand. Power can leak away, sudden. Had to come to terms with their fear.

These worlds don't intersect all that much. They touch, at big pompous entertainments like an Elysée garden party, a fashionable occasion for some big culture-thing. They rub together in the showy restaurants, on the golf course, at exhibitions (the times we've cursed Roland-Garros or the Courson flower show.) A few overlap to some degree, like when bankers and the finance groups are licking there at a fine new honeypot. Come to rub noses at the watering holes, our daily bread and butter all that.

Some types are more Seldom-seen. Not exactly laggards in the money, nor the power-race. Not behindhand in the megalomania ratings either. Narrower frame of reference, lawcourts or the cardiology clinic. The doctors are like that. Do them justice, they often work hard. Great lords in their own shop, and just as far removed from the wear-and-tear. Insulated from servitudes by the string of aides and secretaries whose job is to smooth the path and strew the flower petals. No thought about getting the sack and not keeping up with the mortgage payments, nor even for missing the train, being late for work; boss is looking at his watch, don't let it happen again, Jimmy.

I've never come across anyone like Ray Valdez. Close up, that is. Marky used experts in any branch where he'd got interested. An antiques dealer was just like the international-law specialist; if he wanted a water-diviner he'd tell Patricia to ring up the best.

You can see, straight off, that Raymond is good at his job; intelligent and sensitive, a quality of sympathy and a lot of humour. Be no good as a cop – far too much imagination. Not a bit interested in the chase after money and power, of which I've seen so much. He's more like an artist.

This is a word gets slung about over-lavish and I don't mean pissing in the snow, making casts of the holes. The Marquis is an artist like the juggler in the circus, or a good jockey. I mean the one who sees things we don't. I was trained myself to see a lot others don't, and am no good at defining this. Occasionally though, along the corridors-of-power, I've seen a musician or a painter who was right off the map. I don't understand 'imagination' but they know things which aren't there, not in our world.

You have to have the gift. Some people can tame lions, whisper to horses. I've come to like Ray and I've noticed a few things about him. He doesn't have technical manual skills – but that's another trick word. A skilled touch and he says that's a lot of practice. And discipline; a mass of fears but won't let himself get jumpy.

This attack – he didn't imagine that! Can't think what it's all about, 'he says'. But now he's looking round at every corner and wondering when it's going to hit him next, and I can see he suffers – sure, he laughs that off, and the more credit to him – but if you think you're going to get kneecapped it'll be as painful as the real thing: a doctor, he can see inside his own knee!

Dogged does it; I haven't got beyond the two simple scenarios a cop thinks of. (1) A fellow's got something you want, so you intimidate him into giving it to you. (2) The fellow might do or say something you *don't* want: intimidate him into thinking better of it. But Raymond says that neither or these applies.

Sweet-reason means nothing to a lot of people; the fanatics, the monomaniacs, they've wheels missing. Not loony in any legal sense. Familiar problem; not a lot you can do but be ready; they're apt to be sudden.

An ex-professional respects the professional approach. A government guard sees to it that he's on a good footing with the local *marechaussée*, and where possible that he has also informal contact within. William is quite recently-ex, and these channels are not altogether silted. A place like Strasbourg, Chiefs-of-State, important ministers (and a ruck of attendant politicians) are forever in and out of, and William knows a man in the PJ. The police-judiciaire service is largish here, and important. He does not know the boss; *Le Patron* is ambitious, on the way up, and intent on a good job in Paris. But he does know the chief of staff for that is a man whose local knowledge is valuable and impressive, and tends to stay where he is for several years. Xavier Picarlat is a middle-grade commissaire of much experience and doesn't miss much of what happens in his territory.

"Sure there was a complaint. Proc did nothing with it because it doesn't amount to anything, so there's no instruction, there ain't no witnesses neither. Nothing in that bloody alleyway of course, people are up and down there all day. Fella probably had a goodish idea when your Doctor Valdez would be coming home, wouldn't want to hang around much. Darkish anyhow, rush-hour, nobody saw a thing. So we did a neighbourhood inquiry, likewise zilch, yer-man is well liked, keeps himself to hisself, all correct with his bills and his taxes, not known as heavy drinker or better: or touchy, inclined to argue, unpopular with local teenagers.

"Not thus a local brawl. Where do we go from there?"

"A Funny, maybe? – little boys? No sign of it. Why's he living in a place like that?"

"Artist."

"No law against it, I know of. Brief, couldn't see anything to interest us, meaning it stays on the file but dead in the water. Try the neighbours." He means the political police, interested in Turkish conspirators, Iranian subversives, Albanian Banditry.

"Keep as a rule the grievous-bodily-harm within the Brother-hood."

"True. Well, remember to wash your feet, keeping company with the likes of us."

William has plenty of professional relationships, also a friend or two, and after a fruitless day he went to see Albert, who was gardening; one reason why William feels little enthusiasm for this pursuit, because Albert is so damned meticulous, and his quite large suburban garden is always fiercely impeccable. Albert says things like

'Look before you leap' or 'Fast bind fast find', means them quite literally (little twists of string stowed in his pocket) and William's real
friend is Mrs Martin who is a judge of instruction. But he likes and
respects Albert who is a good man, devotes much time and money to
the poor, is a municipal councillor in Geoffrey de Sainte-Anne's territory (which was how William first met him), is an accountant by
profession, but isn't only the soul of integrity; has very good judgment and an unfailing kindness.

"There," taking due pride in his compost-heap, "lovely out, perhaps we'll have a beer when I'm ready. Bernadette might be late in
that office, she so often is." He took his gloves off to get the phone
out of his pocket. "Good. . . she's on her way. You can stay for
supper? Splendid." He suspects rather that William living alone is
'not properly nourished'.

It's an orderly household. Rather a ceremony of cleaning and polishing tools. Bernadette, the picture of exactitude in the office, is
almost sloppy in her kitchen; a quick-moving energetic woman with
grey hair, good legs, something of a bosom, she has also good judgment: between them, William thinks he'll get good advice, and he's
quite right.

"Why on earth attack this man? Violent, and looks premeditated,
certainly a waylay. Liked, around there: most of them don't even
know he's a doctor, hardly any that he's a Jesuit. That makes no
sense. His professional frequentations, just as preposterous. Intellectual jealousy? – he's getting the credit for my work – utter bullshit." Albert doesn't believe in 'bad language' and would never say
even 'bullshit'. Bernadette hears much worse in the Palais de Justice,
had been called a motherfucker that morning (unlikely though this
seems) said, "This sounds like a fanatic."

"I'd agree there, but on what grounds? Some private belief of his
own? Somebody unbalanced about Jesuits? Or about doctors?"
Albert wiped his mouth, said "Maybe both. Where does Doctor
Valdez stand, for example, on the subject of abortions?"

"Legal termination of unwanted pregnancy," corrected
Bernadette. "A tricky subject, and people get very heated indeed."

"You may have got something there."

"Opens up a number of hypotheses. There is for example euthanasia. Or the move to legalize cannabis in certain therapies. Within the deontology there are several grey areas. We might for instance assume that Doctor Valdez would have unrestricted access to morphia. Which is very far from any supposition that he has made any illegal or even irresponsible use of medicaments."

"But from what you tell us," suggested Albert, "might he have made an unguarded remark? Frivolous, or just ironic. Fanatics have no sense either of humour or proportion."

"Lacking any shred of evidence" in very much the 'judge's voice', "this is vulgar and tendentious speculation, reminds you only to keep your mind alert to different possibilities which may exist. We're going to have supper off the kitchen table."

Dr Valdez hasn't at all made up his mind what – if anything – he can do about William. Essential facts – the wife, and he'll have to talk to Professor Rupprecht. Early days yet. But the Crab – people think of it as slow and lumbering, and so it often is. But one day out in California, where they think about these things, a friend in the Santa Cruz faculty brought him to the beach. He had seen there an extraordinary crab, of phenomenal speed and agility. Put on his mettle he had tried to catch it – the local people laughing heartily at mounting frustration and fury towards the skitter-critter. 'Popularly known as a Sally Lightfoot.' Seen as a lesson, salutary.

It wasn't any affair of Silvia's so that he had rung the Marquis's secretary.

"Joséphine's address? Sure but I have to ask permission; will you hang on?" Then a throat-clearing noise and the Marquis, sounding amused.

"That will be very good for her. And we'll grease the slipway. Patricia will tell her to await you in a proper frame of mind. That will be better than her thinking herself important at your coming to see her. I can't stop for a chat dear boy, I'm rather pressed."

The Santa Cruz campus was in an area 'zoologically interesting'.

"Are there pumas?" he'd asked, impressed.

"Certainly. Saw one the other day out of my bedroom window."

"What was it doing?"

"Drinking out of the swimming-pool." Didn't sound Menacing.

"Do you do anything about that?"

"No. Keep the dogs indoors." Somebody changed the subject, pumas being no cause for excitement hereabouts. Raymond is wondering now what you do if when out for a walk you meet a puma. You'd stay still, wait quietly for it to go away; it's concerned with its own affairs. Supposing it decided it didn't like you? He has no ideas.

The Strasbourg-Paris shuttle is what you'd expect: perfunctory, boring and offensive with chemically perfumed cleansing agents, like a public shithouse. Takes less than an hour but you have to drive out to that horrible airport. Raymond mounted on his donkey in early-morning traffic is content to be unhurried and do some exercises to loosen a stiff neck: the fellow in the car behind would be thinking oh-dear-god, the things they allow out on the roads nowadays. Well then, why doesn't he pass me? Since I'm trundling in the centre lane why does he sit so stupidly behind me? Unforgivable, thus to sink into a morass of footstep-doggers; spies; Assassins. This ghastly man stayed glued to his heels, was next door in the all-day parking lot, behind him at the check-in, herded with him into the waiting-room; destabilizing him.

Climbing aboard the shuttle, with these sinister manifestations about him – now he can't move at all. Dr Valdez slips into the narrative style of the Bloods.

'Boogie grim-lipped passes to the Attack! Obscured by fog the mighty mass of Illtyld looms to starboard. Illtyld the only Tunnel passable by four-motored planes! This is the moment – the pilot glued to his instruments – Blackhawk chooses to launch the deadly assault. . . Blackhawk slim and muscled, embodiment of greeneyed evil, now known to be a WOMAN!

'Has vowed an undying hatred towards Boogie for the rejection of monstrous unnamable Love! Mercifully Orfea the magical musician has foreseen the DEATHTRAP, just as she rejected the evil lesbian love of Blackhawk.' And while regressing comes the childhood query: Why did Orpheus with his lute make trees? It seemed an odd instrument to choose.

A little later in boyhood one tried to put some polish into the narrative. Extremely unconvinced about the sudden rescue of Marina by the Pirates (though these belong to the great-pirate-Valdez, so one has to forgive them.) And why was one reading *Pericles*? Purely on account of it being judged Forbidden to good Catholic school-children because of the Bordel scenes . . .

There isn't even space for his simple stretching exercise. The business-men – instantly pop-crackle-snap went all their locks and lids, and they're all staring at the little plastic screen praying it might tell them something nice. Failing to move his muscles Raymond tries to limber the mind.

The pilot limbers his wires and his wheels. Exhilarating when he turns the power up. But when he gets the go, takes off the brakes and we run, all the brave knights close their visors and sweat inside their armour; they are Afeared and mustn't show it. Whereas Raymond is a professional. Death is simply the hope for a moment of dignity and recollection. 'Into Thy Hands I commend my Spirit'. In the Society we do it every day.

Airborne, it is time to be a Doctor for a moment. He is going to meet William's wife; a step, one hopes, in understanding suggestions. Only the Fellow can cure himself.

Sure. Just like any doctor, he'd passed his exam, got his diploma, the Society threw him straight in to where they knock the Greeny out of you. Six months – about all you can stand, your first tour – with Médecins-sans-frontièrs: the starving-*black*-babies. Dehydration you learn quick. The pill, the needle, if you can find space for it between skin and bone; you know you haven't one chance in a hundred. Your reward? – those amazing luminous eyes of the mother willing you to say You–I–Save. The pill and the needle are of no consequence: what you are is Hope.

I am bloodbrother with William. He said, 'You never know for sure that you will jump to meet the bullet. It's supposed to be the automatic gesture, taking the place of thought. That was the training.'

To be sure: in Africa he had thought of the professional voice, the Jesuit professor in the quiet classroom.

'You are standing in line, in the camp. It is freezing, it is burning: that's no odds. He walked down your line, neither fast nor slow, tapping people. Haircut! – they liked their little cliché jokes. Max Kolbe is said to have made a step to the front, politely. Take me instead – you've only to fill your quota. Could you do that? Think.

'A further fact. Supposing he had been a real SS man. Smart and upright, a man himself dedicated, trained to face death. You could respect that man. He could increase your courage. He might have understood: he would have been capable of saluting you.

'Instead, it was a slob. Didn't look at you, pushed you coarsely by the shoulder – stand over there. Left you no dignity, no self-respect. Death was a dirty ignorant slob with bad-smelling breath.'

Were William condemned, it would be harsh. A forged piece of steel, tough and supple, tempered to hold a fine edge. Into this marvellous raw material have been put much money and time.

These ramblings, since you couldn't call them trains of thought, continued in a limpingly disjointed fashion up to the gates of Paris, at which point Doctor Raymond Valdez disembarked, a bit stiff around the knees but professionally enough, remembering a joke told him by William. Allah sent the Angel of Death to finish with an unpleasant Dictator. The Angel got caught by security guards, was badly beaten up, and sent back in a shocking state. 'My God,' said Allah. 'I hope you didn't tell them who sent you.'

I too, in my turn, am a security guard, here to try and protect William from a cunning, persistent and imaginative assassin.

They knew how to build houses in Baron Haussmann's day. Seeking entry Ray was aware of scrutiny, by the electronic eye. Joséphine – she is alone in the flat – looks rather carefully before letting people into the fortress. A youngish man, doesn't look much like the doctor she has been told to expect; older perhaps than he looks. Expensive clothes, looking rather crumpled. She let him in.

Raymond saw a tall, bony young woman with straight fair hair. Skirt, but would look well in trousers. Large hands and feet, very fine legs (blow your nose and avoid lechery). Living-room, large, well lit, nicely proportioned, Empire furniture, stripy silk upholstery. Plenty of family money. She sat on a chaise-longue, put her legs up to be admired, sat him in a curule chair (surprisingly comfortable).

"Marky has told me about you. Name of Valdez, you Peruvian or something?"

"Something. I'm a famous writer. Nobel Prize, magical realism."

"And a Jesuit – Witchdoctor!" Deep voice, rare in French women.

"Mutter charms. Blow the candle out but put a pinch first of the Devils Foot on the wick – make you see things." Parisian crosschat; if you can't make me laugh you're a bum.

"Come from Strasbourg – provincial puddingdom."

"I hear this all the time – in Paris or London – the world revolves around us; now that Is provincial." She rearranged herself a little pettishly.

"I'm not very clear about this. Come to give me a talking-to, about God?"

"Hardly. God can be a bit of an old fraud now and then."

Laugh, rather a good one, deep in the throat.

"Jesuitical thing to be saying."

"Most doctors would agree that God has a way of not being around when most needed."

"Heresy."

"Just unsentimental. The commonplace claim is that God can't exist, or He wouldn't allow horrible sufferings and injustices. That's to have an over-inflated idea of our importance. Saying that God made a lousy job of it strikes me as arrogant."

"So we are arrogant. As Marky says – I am an entity; they are nonentities."

"How d'you think a doctor survives? Drowned in shit all day. I've no time to feel sorry about the horrors. That's God's business, so I'll get on with my own."

"Man, you are boring me. You've been taking up with William as I hear; that what all this is about?"

"You didn't hear that William's been seen in bad company?"

"Your own, no doubt."

"Better said, the bad company's been seen with William. Little touch of the Crab but awkwardly placed. . . Ah, the Marquis hadn't told you that." She sat upright; the eyes went twice the size.

"Not possible! William. . . but he's the toughest thing out. . . physically. . . He's no age. And all that boxing and volleyball."

"Yes, the crab can be very puritanical about denying us these little pleasures."

"Oh God."

"Oh dear, there's God again."

"That is what Marky meant, making jokes about the Cancer Man, he's talking about you."

"What is it you call him in bed?"

"Jesus, who'll be next? I'm going out today to get my tits X-rayed. I'm going to have a drink and don't tell me it's too early," leaping up and rushing out to the kitchen. She came back with two glasses, pushed the bottle at him. "Open it."

"Madame. . . by the way, my name is Ray," untwisting the wire.

"And a cervical smear. Joséphine will do. What else should I have? That snide remark – that's bloody rude." She took a big swig and it calmed her.

"I am bloody rude. This the best you can do, getting in a fuss?"

"Oh all right. Slight shock, someone you know."

"That sounds accurate, as far as it goes. Your turn to pour."

"I've got this nasty feeling you'll be on about God again if I'm not careful. Well, I am careful. I care also about William."

"But you don't love him, is that what you're telling me?"

"Not at all. I did, or thought I did. I was mistaken. A clear conscience, about that. I tried."

"Yes, it's a word to be careful with. 'In all conscience' we say, or perhaps 'speaking as a conscientious woman'. Tcha, if the human being were something we could pour water in at the top, and be satisfied when urine comes out at the bottom, we could treat illness with a few plants, champagne for instance. Could you say why, do you think, or don't you know?"

"He's much too good." Quite sadly and seriously. "It drove me bats. I'm not good at all. I wanted to claw him." There would be more, plenty more . . . but it was a moment of lucidity.

"Like the man said, daylight and champagne could not be clearer. Not too sure about the daylight nowadays."

"The champagne isn't what it was either. One thought life would be more fun, somehow."

"I didn't come here to pester you. Only to know where you stood. Then I know where I stand. I'll take myself off."

"We could have lunch together. If you liked." And that too told him something. He'd have enjoyed it too; this girl with the lovely long legs. 'I am tempted, Scaramouche' and the answer come pat – 'Always yield to temptation, master.' Sadly, life isn't simple any more. Nice little place round the corner, let's have coffee back at home, and you can spend the afternoon in bed with her. "Back on the shuttle?" she asked. "I see. But I rather imagine you'll be back."

"Paris is not far." And the distance is speedily lessened.

A tormenting female. Just the sort the Marquis would like. So he thought about the old man, while banging through the lunchtime traffic saying 'It's time for the apéro.' Meaning that he should stop for lunch.

The old man was making a virtue of being old. 'Can't be bothered with all this computer bullshit.' Internets and e-mails; accepts that life has gone past him, but trying hard still to enjoy girls.

Raymond hasn't felt frightened since being in Paris; hadn't had time? Too much else on his mind: himself is not important enough.

When younger he had known and greatly loved an old lady. Russian; a poet, along with much else. Long after he had lost sight of her he had learned that when coming towards the end of her life she had written memos of people she had known, and among them himself. By now Doctor Valdez is quite high on self-awareness, reckons he knows himself pretty well. In that script, a few pages of scrawly handwriting, was a passage he thought summed-up the matter.

'He was a type one has known more of, afraid only of being afraid. It is good to see a young man in love with his own honour. He accused himself of physical cowardice; full of a reckless nervous courage. He said once that if he saw a man, or even a child, fallen in the Seine he would be frightened to jump in. The speed of imagination is such that he saw himself drowning while incapable of saving another, since he was a poor swimmer. Adding that he wouldn't jump in the Seine anyhow since any doctor knows the extent of chemical and bacteriological hazard. I told him that he would have gone in to a fire. No no, he said; afraid of pain. I treated that with contempt. He would laugh at pain, and even while shouting for morphia. Proud as Satan, what he could not bear was that another should think him afeared.' Not a bad reading, one would admit.

He has been thinking about words – 'Sweet of you' he'd said to her invitation. In French *gentil* but the English would not say 'gentle of you'. Miss Joséphine is not very sweet, but she has her gentle side. The Marquis would probably add that gentility had nothing to do with being a gentleman (a word the French associate with good manners); he enjoys these 'little phrases'.

The airport check-in girl has not her mind on her work. Her little radio was only mouthing commercials.

"What is it?"

"Crash on the autoroute," managing to be distant, rude and patronizing in those few syllables. Tornado in Arkansas, mass destruction, hundreds homeless, but on the midday news it's 'Is that all?' On the Western Front, nothing to report; General Haig is said to be preoccupied. Here, now, is a police mouthpiece saying (being French) that a certain-number-of-questions have been raised, calling-for-clarification. Quite. Such as, why are human beings inhuman? Ray crawls into a corner, suffering from depression.

Before the flight was even called he has heard it all from the neighbours. Chap overtaking, another has the same idea; big truck brakes too hard and goes crossways; six more go barrelling straight into him. Before you can say Air Bag. Yes and it could have been me. But not in the Café de Commerce, which is here. 'What I always say Is. . .' The poor lunk who suggests people ought to drive slower is howled down by Our Individual Liberties.

La France Moisie; it will translate as musty, mouldy, mildewed. Never quite submerged. Much is submerged, much of the time, so that nobody ever quite knows how much there really is. But a lot. It was happy through most of the nineteenth century; perturbed by 1848 – much more by the Commune. The twentieth was less good: it is still having a dreadful time trying to hold down the memory of '40 to '44. Mildew-France hates everyone but particularly Jews, blacks, Brits, Germans, the neighbours, Europe, and the State. Doctor Valdez, like all his profession, can put his sense of smell in abeyance at will, more or less, but there's a fearful stink in the afternoon shuttle.

Quite a different atmosphere from this morning (heavy with the sense of doom, guillotines-at-dawn). This crowd got it Done-by-lunchtime, hilarious when the Presentation went well; not going back to the office, neither: boss expects you to be on call up to eleven at night, and fuck that. Raymond's neighbour is chatty. Asked his racket Ray says 'Endocrinologist' but this stopper does not always work. His new-pal gets into athletics, alarmingly. 'These Tour de France riders, stuff they have, dope no? Increase your red corpuscles, doesn't show up in the weewee.' Raymond to his sorrow knows about this, is led (to the greater) to speak of it. To make it work you inject a lot of iron, more than the metabolism copes with. By the end of your career you've a simply lovely little liver-cancer all set up and waiting for you. No, he doesn't know what can be done about it.

Discontent; certainly thinking Endocrinwhatsit, all worn out from getting his golf handicap down.

"Just settling into our landing pattern," said the loudspeaker. Crossing the Mont Saint Odile, famous in myth and history. A shuttle once chose to crash here. Middle of the night, of the winter, of thick forest, of deep snow; inconvenient. After many-many boards of enquiry there was still nobody who knew why.

Bump, whizz. "There's no point in Rushing," said the stewardess. Quite as usual, Raymond cannot recollect where he has left the car.

An ordinary day, filled with violence – roads, planes, people – but no more than usual. Not going to squawk like a jay but inclining to gibber, Raymond went to the office. Silvia – fat, lovely, comforting, competent – knows him in this state, shields him from an evil world. When he jerks out 'Tea' like that, and shuts himself in the stuffy little office (before you get to the air scrubbed and filtered) she obeys. Tea green and gunpowdery is stowed in a padded basket. He won't come out, and she'll let nobody in.

Doctor Valdez Consults. In the polite world of medicine, formal and *protocolaire*, tight-mouthed about fees undeclared to nosy tax officials, this is well understood. Idea-man. What – today's topic – do athletes mean by 'form'? Dope left aside (boring topic at best) what makes a footballer score goals, a skier gain a yard of speed, a tennis player see the ball earlier?

What makes William Barton, so harmonious a figure in that extravagant Paris household, so disjointed here upon a bed of roses? The Crab had reached out, given him a nip. That can happen to anyone but there's more than an extraordinary chance.

The wife; one always suspects the wife, but Valdez is wary of an argument that facile. A football trainer buys a player; a wonderful talent costing millions. Everything points to his fitting in perfectly – and he turns out utterly useless; sullen, awkward and unhappy. The wife – but no; there isn't any wife.

William had felt himself bought?

This woman; had she invested too much – never mind the money – of hope and delight and pride? That this marriage should turn so sour after so few months, leaving a cancer lodged in William's gut, and who could tell what bitter misery in hers – that is not only an evil and unhappy chance.

There's a factor, Valdez, that you would prefer to disregard. Just tell me, would you, why you found this woman so sudden and so violent an intoxication?

You ran like a rabbit. Five more minutes and you'd have been propped there on your back legs with your eyes gone glassy, while the predator danced. About to make a meal of you, whenever it shall choose.

Part Two

You don't need these Vast quantities of water. Enough for it to swim in. You put a little salt, a splosh of oil, stops it sticking. Keep the pot boiling quite gently, stir it with a fork so the strands stay loose, respect the time it says on the packet. Choose thick spaghetti, not that skinny stuff, this is number-seven.

They are together in Raymond's flat. William has invited himself to dinner. Asking for a cookery lesson; things for when you live by yourself and are sick of sardines off the corner of the table.

"I only know about ten things, oh all right, twenty. But I do those really well. My spaghetti is Famous," preening ostentatiously.

"I'm writing it all down," said William humbly.

They've already made the Bolognese. ('I know four ways but this is the easiest.') Demonstration of this great brilliance. Only cooks and doctors have a really sharp knife.

"Difference is that cooks don't sterilize it. Wash your feet but not the rice. Learn to be a bit dirty."

"What kind of cheese?"

"Oh I don't know, Czech Emmenthaler. Parmesan is for when you keep it separate. This you strew over, and we'll bake it in the oven, all gold and crunchy. There. About a quarter of an hour. Time now to have a real drink. While we make the salad." All sorts of greenery. "Good for your bowels," said Dr Valdez.

"I have to take my pill."

"Yes, poor you. Filthy chemicals. Let's see. You aren't really supposed to drink, with this, but we pay no attention. I'm going to get you off all these pills. Little girl instead to massage you. Spray you with cold water so you don't get the horn. Right, let's lay the table." William said, "This is good. Oh Yaysus-Gott. Give me some more. Three star." Wiping his mouth for a long drink of red plonk.

"I've never been to a real three-star restaurant."

"I have and often. My masters, getting in was one of our perks. Monsieur-le-Marquis was addicted to them. Liked his tumtum. You say then, thank you Baby-Jesus in the little red velvet waistcoat."

"It's immoral to spend a month's wage on a meal."

"Yes, that's what's so nice when it's free. You're right, these people are awful. Caillera." A good word. Backslang for riff-raff.

"Green tea tomorrow. Vegetables and fruit, I'm taking you off meat. Fish, but not the Bar en croûte Sauce Choron."

"You sound like a judge of instruction."

"Proust remarked that in a priest as in an alienist – and I'm a bit of both – you will find something of the judge of instruction."

"This is you working for me. Now," said William seriously, "here is me working for you. Let's have a talk about the fellow who busted you."

"You setting up as my guard?"

"I'll do the exercises you prescribe. Physically limber. Mentally too – your damn Jane. Not 'Guard' – that's a monarchist word we refuse."

"If not a guard," said Ray, "then perhaps an angel".

William had been struck by the simplicity of the flat.

"This your vow of poverty?" teasing him.

"Nonsense." Ray rather cross. "Everything I want, and in perfect comfort. I like it this way. I'm afraid I don't pay much attention to vows of poverty."

"Nor chastity? I rather thought not. She left a lipstick in the bathroom."

"Ay de mí. The police are on my track. . . That's Janine."

"I know how to be discreet," said the angel," and I intend also to know the joker who clonked you, and why."

"Really," rather helpless. "I know very little about Janine."

"But one can find out."

"I'm sure you can. . . Dumas says somewhere 'It isn't always the one with the key who enters the house'." Raymond was feeling the same sudden exhaustion as attacks him when there is a violent meaningless quarrel with Janine whom he loves and can't help it.

One passes through the world, knowing scarcely anything – probably nothing important – about people who are intimate friends. There used to be a euphemism, 'intimacy' meaning you'd slept together. Now they just 'have sex' which is about as intimate as being squashed together on a rush-hour train. Not Ray though.

Somebody at a 'party' had put on an old Kansas-City record and Ray said 'Lovely thing'.

'So you like a Beeg swing band' said the girl taunting him. 'Isn't that a bit antediluvian? Benny Goodman in all his pomp?'

'No no that's just loud. Vitality but crude, noisy, obvious, incurably vulgar.' He was drunker than he thought.

'Oh I do so agree. I do so love Ellington.'

'Like my father. My grandfather too, probably. Conveys thought, that'll never do nowadays.'

'Pom de pom pom' singing the piano chords of a famous introduction. Yes, back when it started in 1940 'Take the A-train' had been soft and relaxed – tender.

But this was the Count; the bounce he gives the orchestra has the lightness – swift, airborne, articulate – she was still there.

'The Count – Freddy Green – Walter Page – Jo Jones; you've the best rhythm section there ever was.'

'Add in the Prez' with her eyes shining.

'So let's go home and listen to Lester.' As a master of slipping sliding piano chords says – 'Maybe it happens this way'.

"Whose house was the party?" asked William.

"Roger. Is his name Blessington? – doesn't sound quite right."

Doctor Roger was quite easy; a big jovial man with a general practice, wide among the Council-of-Europe crowd because he speaks good English (he is English; name of Pilkington). A man with golf clubs in the back of the car and pills in the pocket for all occasions, a man who makes you feel better straight away. He thought he knew Janine but rather-thought the name sounded wrong.

"Not one of my patients." It's going to be one of those days, William told himself, when everyone has another name. "If it's the one I'm thinking of. Decorative girl but have it in my mind she's called Mireille. Wait a moment, did she come accompanied – well sorry, it was that kind of gathering." With a sudden shrewd glance, "I know now but I didn't say this, it doesn't do to repeat gossip so you didn't hear it from me; it was PermRep."

William is quite at home in this world. Strasbourg is one of the diplomatic cities. What with the Council, the Parliament, floods of Funcs, Ministers forever popping in and out, Community countries have accredited missions here, the Permanent Representatives with a vaguely ambassadorial status. This one has an exalted view of his own importance; the name of PermRep attaches to him. Dr Barbour (doctorate of what? – nobody knows) is a tall thin man of much grey-ish distinction. His teeth and fingernails glitter, the lenses of his glasses flash like lasers, his shirts are very white and the cuffs show off long flexible busy hands; a silvery tie goes with his hair and he has suits the colour and texture of cigar-ash. Oh yes and he's a secret football-fan. William finds out a lot more but most of it irrelevant.

William doesn't lurk and neither does he stalk; it gets noticed. Incompetent and illegal, and he has no intention of disturbing Doctor Holier-than-thou – or not for the moment; that's the fellow would be quick to make a complaint and he's no longer a serving cop: status dodgy. He'll pounce though, on poor 'Mireille'. A grin there, thinking of the Marquis, one of whose techniques was getting names wrong. 'You – Francine – or are you Muriel?'. She's easy to spot; the studio (that's what they call a one-room flat) is in the Robertsau quarter for 'prestige' and she has a little Spider, Italian racing red, old but bold. She's also very pretty – really Ray has good taste, he thinks when she looms. He looms too, large and cop-like.

"Now my girl, you're being conspicuous. You've been attracting my attention."

"Who are you? Oh – you're some sort of police."

"Putting it in a nutshell. You can call it that."

"I don't believe a word of it." The card with the tricolour stripe in a little plastic folder is old but has been genuine.

"Less backchat, girl, unless you want to be brought down to the House."

"No. I have to do my shopping."

"What you need my dear is a talking-to, so we'll just walk into this café here where it's nice and quiet, and drink a cup of their delicious coffee."

"I'm not your dear and keep your hands off me."

"Quite enough that you're Doctor Barbour's dear. . . Now that's diplomacy for you. Important foreign power, authority is sensitive to such things." When you pounce make it a good one and be sure it'll stick. "It won't do, my dear." Paternally, dislodging, sitting her down. She is not about to scream.

Continuing to fix her with the eye – Two coffees please miss. – William is about to switch on the kindness but makes sure of the demolition first. Janine has taken a cigarette out of her bag and is lighting it, giving herself a countenance. Thinking.

"What's he been saying? He's got no cause for a complaint."

"Nothing, he's made no complaint. But you'll do well not to ask. You're also very friendly with another doctor – eminent research scientist."

"That's right, we're friends."

"Quite so, you clean his flat for him and leave your lipstick in the bathroom."

"Is that where it got to? – I thought I'd lost it." Perky.

"Understand this little chat" getting omens into the voice, "Somebody attacked Doctor Valdez outside his house. Nasty thing that was and we want to know more about it. Now would you want me to dress you up a Verbal-Process? Make you eat it too, and without any mayonnaise."

"No truly I know nothing about it. Please, that's the truth."

"So you can tell me the nothing in detail, for as long as it takes, if need be we'll eat lunch here together. Each pays his own" with the tiger-shark smile.

Like all European towns Strasbourg is made up of villages. The old walled city was also moated; and a loop of water – the Faux Rempart – was led around and rejoins the river Ill, making quite a distinctive passage over to the 'new' town built in the nineteenth century. Indeed the river splits into several streams which meander before tipping themselves into the Rhine, dividing land areas each with a little village centre of its own. Until 1945 the city came to an end at the canal which links the Rhine to the Marne, rather a bold engineering feat. Here, bordering the waterway, they put the complex of quite hideous buildings which make up the Palace of Europe and house the Parliament, the Council, the Court of Human Rights; all of it peopled by a monstrous swarm of bureaucrats. The grandest of these functionaries found themselves housing in the pleasant villa district surrounding. Minor funcs had nowhere to go until they crossed the canal and invaded the village immediately beyond; this is the Robertsau.

It was known, famous, for the quality of alluvial soil which had built up a bank between the marshy bits; it was Strasbourg's market garden. Since it is no distance cartloads came daily, beautifully fresh, to the city markets, along with chickens, and fish from the river.

William's authority for these historic details is of course Albert, a real Strasbourgeois who remembers these good times.

A horrible change has overtaken this peaceful and civilized area. The speculating builders offered the price-you-can't-resist to the small farmer, drowned the little fields of carrots and onions under a flood of concrete and threw up desirable-residences for funcs who could afford much higher rents than other people, and were pleased to find themselves handily placed for the job. The Robertsau gardens are now dinky apartment blocks with 'standing', a French word meaning nasty-but-expensive. People like Janine live there in cramped conditions but happy to have an address with prestige. . . There are a few old houses remaining, and the church, but the main street is now the bus route out to La Wantzenau where the chickens used to come from, and is choked with diesel exhaust. As for the carrots they all come now from Morocco.

And even the pubs have become tea-shoppes with little calorie-reduced menus for the weight-watching func wives.

William worked on this girl. It wouldn't occur to him to say 'hard'. A professional would know what he means when he says 'Could do with a drink'. No need to explain, he has turned her inside-out like a glove.

He sat back, caught the waitress's eye and said *"Un quart de rouge."*

"A what?"

"Un pichet. Anything but Bordeaux."

"We don't have little jugs, we've only bottles." This is the point (Albert would have said) of explaining how an honest village becomes a toffee-nosed suburb. There must be a real pub left somewhere for the old men to play cards in, but you'd have to know where to find it.

"Oh all right then, a glass. What have you got?"

"Hold on then," said Janine in a very small voice. "I could do with one myself."

"What d'you want?" asked Kind Uncle.

"What I was thinking, d'you know, suppose we were to share a bottle of crémant." Alsace champagne, and when good can equal the stuff from Reims. It won't be that good here but it won't be that naughty price either.

"Right" said William, "and bring two menus". Now he's in a way to get a few things straight and more reliably: Janine can't open her mouth without lying but now they're beginning to understand one another. It's much too grand to talk about Stockholm syndrome but the principle is the same; a kind of human relationship begins to instil itself. If, interrogating people, you can get to a point where they begin to find you sympathetic, you can do without a lot of threats and bullying. You've some idea of the level of disbelief applicable, and you've a little list of the facts and opinions you want to verify. And if you're William this is the moment to gain her confidence.

Raymond Valdez

Janine has vanished. Janine doesn't live here any more. I've rung her number, got the machine, left a word. No reaction. I know what that means. I'm not going to ask any questions.

'I only know that he who forms a tie is lost. The germ of corruption has entered into his soul.' Epigraph to a Greene book. A good writer; nobody like him at throwing the noose around your neck. Old Hangman Greene.

I am a Jesuit? A consecrated man? Awful word, next door to castrated. No wonder that people see one as a weirdy. A suspected pederast. I can be respected, even admired, but at the back of their minds I am a poor thing, unable to love or fulfil a woman. I'm like anybody else. I am Monsieur Tout-le-Monde.

The French like to think about God from time to time. They like to be baptized; that's a piece of insurance. To be married in church, as well as the town-hall. More respectable, though it won't make the marriage last longer. And if possible, to be scraped clean by the curé when dying. Allaying fear with a dose of pious sentimentality. Praying is an incantation, helpful in hard times. Rather like the old Bovril advertisement. 'Buoys up that sinking feeling.'

I am aware that I made promises, among others a vow of celibacy. It is no excuse to say that I never believed in it much. The arguments seemed to beg the question. The early Church didn't bother about it much. Avoid Fornication: yes, quite.

I need no telling that adultery is the worst of human conditions. Very well; one has a mistress – rather like Mr Greene.

No sensible bishop ever threw out the curé for having a mistress; he'd get left with the pederasts. There are celibate men, to be sure. Yes, and a house full of them is a nasty sight. Smelly, too.

Raymond, you are behaving badly. Like a small child. I do not mind your being ignoble but do not be irresponsible. Please call to mind the simple truths you tell your patients. You can treat their symptoms: they must find their therapy. Look your emotional upheavals in the eye.

Like the mathematician said: 'God exists because mathematics are coherent, and the Devil exists because we can't prove it.'

Had there ever been an age of innocence? Couldn't remember any, even in boyhood. Only of inexperience, when energy was unbounded and everything so easy; of violent horseplay and word-games.

'Think of a triad. Got to be three and have a magical, a poetical rhythm. An incantation.'

'Right, and last one out's a sissy. Freeman Hardy and Willis.'

'Timothy Whites and Taylor.'

'Bristol Myer and Squibb.'

'Smith French Kline.'

'Not very good, that. London Midland and Scottish.'

'Ha. Atchison Topeka and Santa Fé.'

'Denver and Rio Grande'.

'Cheating, that's only two. Baltimore and Chesapeake.'

'Er – Hugli, Haug and Hammerschmidt.'

'What?'

'Eminent firm of Swiss notaries in Zürich.'

'You just made them up.'

'Fiction is better than reality, sissy.'

So it is, thought Raymond, looking around at his bookshelves. '*In omnibus requiem*' – though this is somebody quoting some other old bugger – 'In everything I sought rest and never found it save in a corner with a book'. But I love Janine. This suggestion of William's that she – even as a catspaw – fills me with horror.

We had zest then. Pleasure was intense, in the tiniest of joys – and as for adultery. . . we took a romantic view of classical tragedy. Tristan and Iseult. Lancelot and Guinevere. If comic, then like the young boy in *La Ronde* who gives a great jump in the air, says with huge relish 'I am the lover of a married woman!' Whoopee.

Janine at least wasn't going to appear with a little bundle wrapped in a shawl. There's that, nowadays: it isn't much but it's something.

There isn't anything vicious about her, thought William. Sees herself as 'Belle de Jour' – a French actress famous for her beauty playing a woman whose fantasies about sex lead her to volunteer for the bordel; talented part-time amateur, complicated longings for humiliations and punishments. Janine, he rather thinks, prefers these to remain imaginary. The Marquis giggling mightily at Belle, had probably slept with her himself. ('Why not? Everyone else has') But it's a fair guess that Janine isn't any real whore. The attraction about Ray at the start might well be his 'apartness'. Jesuit after all, not supposed to sleep with women. Brilliant physician would make it the more exciting. Poor girl then find herself in love with him? Mm, she both is and isn't.

Hard not be unfair. She *liked* Raymond. Quite; Dr Valdez is attractive, amusing – fun to be with. Also very generous: has plenty of money though not very good at collecting it; better at giving it away. This is pretty heaven-sent for Janine who is always broke and a practised borrower. It's easier to forget debts when the lender forgets too.

Valdez has, however casual and negligent, social standing. Knows all sorts of people, many rich and influent. A girl like this is impressed, and on the make in a small way. 'Don't you know any television producers?' You never know, it might lead to a job, a step up, however tiny that's precious when you're forever on the scrabble. She probably wouldn't know about the Marquis, since if Ray is discreet at all he is so about patients, but she's an astute picker-up of gossip, name-dropper, weaver-in of little hints and fragments. 'Ray was laughing about Joey who can't speak his lines without the teleprompter to feed him' and from there it's a small step to inventions – 'Joey was saying only last week' with a little disclaimer, 'No, no, I don't know him all that well'. Her struggle to get off the outermost fringe of show biz.

But there is an honest simplicity to Janine, also. Affection first because he's kind and considerate. She was touched by the little marks of his dependence upon her: he is lonely and he loves her. He is touchingly ready to believe she has talent, given a chance to an opening. (Useless as an actress but a good dancer and can sing a bit). Eager, hard worker, confident with the jargon of lighting or photography; she picks up a living, in and out of little parts. She loves him. Or so she thinks, and so he thinks. Sometimes it's even true and she has made sacrifices for him.

And she is of course good in bed.

There's more, which he isn't going to find out in just one morning. Openings in the secretive defence mechanisms. Since she gets into bed with PermRep. But the Robertsau pub is no place for learning more about that. Janine being tearful in public could create a problem. She's fairly well known 'in the village'. And the very last person (here or anywhere else) Janine's going to talk about will be PermRep. Who is very guarded indeed, personally as professionally.

Instinct, a cop-instinct, tells William to steer well clear of the Permanent Representative. A prominent personage. A political personage. You do not meddle with the affairs of this sort of man. Woe betide you if you do. William has known it happen. There have been police officers; ambitious, zealous, eager to pursue corruption where suspected. Mysterious things happened to them; they could find themselves disgraced, destroyed: a career broken.

He felt pretty sure, now, that what happened to Ray Valdez was along these lines. But a physical attack – that was uncharacteristic. More likely would be some massive smear upon a reputation. Upon a doctor, some accusation difficult to disprove; that he dealt in drugs, illegal abortions. . . Smashing him up seemed oddly crude. But Janine had been given a huge fright. That might be the idea. Careful, girl. Getting the nose broken – could happen to you.

You find something out, and you reach a barrier, telling you that you aren't getting any further. When this happens you think about it, and perhaps you find out what your friends think about it.

Bernadette and Albert Martin are good friends. Of good counsel, and so they should be, since she is a judge and he is an accountant of whom people say, 'Shrewd you know, a long-headed chap.'

An investigating magistrate does not preside over a tribunal but is next door. Their job is to decide whether there is a case to answer: it is the first and perhaps the most important filter in the judicial process. They can be very good; and sometimes they are very bad. The young ones have often clean shining ideals about law and justice. 'In such a world as this' she says after twenty-five years of experience 'an idealist – perhaps it's only a sentimentalist – must be stoned to death'.

"Oh my dear boy. . ." Those famous words, that judgment be justice, administered 'without fear or favour'. . . "I could dine out for a year, on what I hear in a week." The obligation to secrecy, and the Palais leaks like a sieve. The private lives of the Bench! The police, undermanned and undertrained. And as for lawyers. . . "Principles of good and evil are totally irrelevant. I am there to serve the Law. God asks of us to do our daily work; everything else is sentiment." To suggest cynicism would be ludicrous. Instructing judges are mostly firm believers in sending people to prison while awaiting trial, often for months on end. Keeps them safe and cools their heels. An admission of guilt will come the readier. It is notorious around the Palais that Madame Martin never sends anybody to prison if she can possibly help it.

In Strasbourg there's a smack, still, of the independent mind. Betimes French and betimes German, and people have never taken kindly to either. As though a faint memory persists of being a free-imperial-city, tyrannized by bishops, distressed by local nobilities, periodically besieged-burned-plundered by warlords, remaining bloodyminded. Here you find the 'Steckelburger', an old boy with a stick and a funny hat, who stumps about poking his nose into everything and complaining about it. He knows where the beer is best and the *tarte-flambée*; he is scathing about the municipal authority and the football team. Albert is imbued with this antique civic spirit.

'My young friend,' he calls William.

For the young man has remarkable qualities. A great pity to see him at a loose end like this. Police officers are hopeless intriguers and many are crooks. But the Protection Service was élite material. One had little respect for their masters – politicians! – but plenty for those who looked after them. Ideals, devotion: shocking to see that go to waste. This wife – frivolous and irresponsible young woman. Illness is a dreadful misfortune to a young man in splendid physical condition. One may hope: Rupprecht is well known to be a good doctor. People say things like 'avoid worry'. Just the thing to make you worry. Mr Martin fulminates against many things which worry him. This is a dreadful country. What have we done to deserve it?

"I know some prosecutors," said Bernadette pouring herself a cup of coffee, "almost as nasty as Albert".

"Yes, well, I was thinking of this man William has mentioned, the Permanent Representative. I've come across him. Be very prudent in dealings there. A lot of power, a long arm. I'm not concerned with an important foreign country, so-called friendly, with that great taste for meddling in the affairs of others, but with the man himself. I know something of him. A rigid character, one of those who has always to be in the right, superciliously dismissive of any opinion but his own. Doesn't do to get on the wrong side of him."

Bernadette has a legal liking for Latin citations.

'*Dejiciat potentes de sede.*' He throws down the mighty from their seat."

William knows this one; it's from the Psalms; it was a favourite with the Marquis. He knows the literary reference that goes with it, which – typically – the old man was fond of acting, with empressment and much relish.

'Among the best pages Dumas ever wrote. Henry the Third's brother has just died miserably – thoroughly deserved – and the King laments: Who then will succeed me? Upon the very moment the doors fly open. Dramatic announcement – His Highness, Monseigneur le Duc de Guise!' The old boy loving it. Probably an ancestor of his. 'The duke sees the deathbed and goes down on his knees, in the presence of God and the King. Magnificent. And Chicot quotes that splendid line – 'He shall throw down the mighty from their seat.' It amused William. Marky was fond of dukes – they were all his cousins!

"I'm accustomed to these people, Albert. I'm not afeared of your lousy fascist."

"But you'll be careful, dear boy."

"Feel sure of it."

What he found, or better said dragged out into daylight, while looking into Janine, was a pal of hers, young woman going by the name of Iñez. Real name Thomasina, some antenatal confusion, she was supposed to be a boy, but that's no name to build a career upon. And a real peasant. Would talk but only for money. Yes and no and perhaps, and haven't heard, can't say. They've learned in childhood to act dim. And he has nothing with which to twist her arm.

"If you were to put me on the payroll then." Convinced he's from the Ministry, and can cough up some of the *'sonnante et trébuchante'* (which is French for chinking twinkling mint sauce). She reckons that he'll threaten but won't do anything, will get fed-up and start offering cake, thinking that he'll get on better being kind. So he will, but it better be real cake.

These ones are all the same, thought William. The day they were born they learned how to tap the electricity bypassing the meter. Aged four they were pinching cake from the baker. Aged six, shoplifting in the supermarket.

William found himself, since nothing's-for-free-mister, with just one hard item, and that wrung out, since Janine had let something slip: occasionally – v-e-r-y occasionally when things are really tight, these girls make a little bit on the side, courtesy of Madame Bénédicte. He has heard the name before.

Oddly enough, from his ex- or nearly-ex brother-in-law, Geoffrey de Sainte-Anne. In an unbuttoned moment, in the company of the excellent spätlese Riesling. The Baron had also his little moment of weakness now and then, in which Madame Bénédicte specializes. She has a most appropriate address, just opposite the convent of the Bon Pasteur, where the holy nuns used to look after delinquent girls. 'I say old boy, you'll be discreet about that.'

As close of mouth of Iñez he finds the lady, but a lot more sophisticated since very well protected indeed; not just by a PermRep but the entire machine, Parliament, Commission, Council, diplomatic immunity all round. Interpol have now also their data-base in Strasbourg.

Madame offers coffee which smells so good he hates to refuse. Madame also hates to refuse, but really Monsieur, you can't expect anything else.

"Seeing it's you. . . I'm trying to think whether I know of any little things which. . . Iñez – what's the other one called? Rings no bell. Did she perhaps come with a word from Monsieur Philippe? We're caterers you know, when there's a big banquet one can't be always too choosy about extra waitresses. Helps out now and again with the decorations. He has this little shop on the quays. Do give my regards to the Baron."

A nice Renaissance house, a dark little shop you'd never notice. Grilles on the windows and behind them pieces of jewellery cunningly lit. It hadn't been easy to find.

Indeed he wondered why he'd been given this much. Bénédicte the table-turner. Tells fortunes, you know. Maybe she'd seen in the Tarot that Monsieur Philippe was about to meet a Dark Lady.

Habit, and training; study and outside too. Quite a lot of effort had gone into this already. No name to the shop, but a nice logo of a double L intertwined. In Versailles that stands for the Sun King. In a formal square for Lucien Lelong, formerly a well known couture house, made very good perfume. This is in between; classy rather. An air of money being made, discreetly so. The police had been no real help; Xavier merely saying, 'Someone we'd like to know more about'. Well, always willing to oblige a friend. He looked at the door, which was metal-sheathed and heavy; swung well-balanced but would lock itself with a distance-touch. Inside was dark after the street but lit up a lot of dark blue velvet when the door went tingaling. And a little man smiling affably came in from the back which was strongly lit behind the velvet curtain and gave a glimpse of a jeweller's workshop. And both summed the other up in a quick practised glance. One big man smooth and blank (and looking slow) in a nice Lanvin suit, very nice Sulka tie. One small man with an apron over a baggy cardigan but carried the neck poked forward as though the collar hurt at the back; a long sloping cropped head and the scalp at the forehead seemed too large for the skull, wrinkling and contracting. A pity William never reads a book because Ray Valdez would have given his yelp of laughter. Gagool!

"Now how may I help you?" Affable's not the word. Carneying.

"Sorry to interrupt," in a Bertie Wooster voice, "but I'm looking for Iñez". And knew instantly that he had the right address because in that instant Gagool looked out of the humble eyes.

"Who's that? Sorry," with a wave of humble hands, here we have jewellery.

"If I say so myself, extremely fine. Not the Place Vendôme, you'll say – my colleagues. I don't pay their rents, you don't pay their prices. Now I can see, you're a man women will find attractive. Shall I make some suggestions?" The hands are striking; small, thin, white; flexible.

William did his broad open smile. "Iñez," he said, friendly. The eyes didn't react a second time.

"My dear sir, we aren't understanding each other. I speak six languages."

"One will do. Iñez."

"We seem to be at cross-purposes."

"No." And the change was sudden, complete, satisfying.

"Mess with me, friend, you'll go where the woodbine twineth." The fast white hand scuttled across the dark blue velvet, quick as a fleeing spider. It reappeared as suddenly, holding a pistol. "I'd recommend that you leave. At once, quietly, for good." William maintained the fixed idiot grin.

"Put it away. Dangerous toy." The man did something with his foot and the lock of the door gave a soft snap. With his other hand he reached below the counter, came up with a telephone.

"I think we'll have some police."

"Are you sure you wish to draw attention to yourself?" The eyes studied him for a long ten seconds. They protruded a little, hard and opaque, seeming polished. Perhaps beady was the word.

"I wish to know something simple," said William. "Who attacked a friend of mine. And who paid for it. Could have been you. More likely someone you hired. At whose suggestion?" The man smiled suddenly, gaily. The pistol went away, as smoothly as it had appeared.

"For holdup artists," in a polite way. "And that you aren't.

"You're something else. A busybody. A nosy parker. We deal with them in a different way." He moved sideways from behind the counter with neat small steps, stood facing William on the soft-carpeted floor. Nicely polished black shoes, a little apart, the neck still stretched forward, the mouth pursed up as though to whistle; the arms loose and the hands in the trouser pockets. Kind of you, thought William, to give me so much warning. Perhaps the intent is sadistic: he's enjoying this.

'We teach them a lesson. We cut them open." The hand came up to waist height and the knife-blade clicked. "A clear case of self-defence, my dear sir. He menaced me with his fists. Little me." This is a cliché but knife fighters do it; they sway from side to side. The effect is supposed to be like a snake, intimidating. In William's book snakes are timid creatures and run away. If you tread on them they bite you. A straightforward transaction and he has had hours of patient training. Martial arts, they're called. He's a little out of training. Never mind, the adrenaline will flow when needed. He threw the right arm out and up, the left hand hooking in and down. Feinting the jab and cross counter southpaw. Good, the speed is still there.

The left hand got the wrist. He brought up a knee and banged the knife hand on it hard. The knife jumped and fell on the carpet. The open right hand came in and slapped the face: one tries not to clonk them across the ear, which might cause damage. Perhaps it wasn't quite hard enough because the face jerked back and spat, right on a nice clean shirt. He had still his grip on the wrist, which he twisted and brought up into the small of the back, turning the man round. Cross because of the spit William pushed hard. The man lurched quite roughly into a table and fell down.

When we fought with the thick canes we had masks and padded clothing. They still hurt, considerably. But we didn't spit at one another. William picked up the knife and closed it, went round the counter and collected the pistol; had now all the weaponry that had been on view: there might be more but it wasn't a worry.

"Pick yourself up. Now you answer my question." The man got up and backed away but he wasn't hurt.

"You'll get nothing out of me. We'll meet you again, and I'll know you, and there'll be no witnesses." Of a sudden William felt pain, sharp and insistent, inside him.

"I see, or I hear, anything of you, little man, ever – ever – when the PJ picks you up there'll be traces of heroin in your pockets. You'll be done for possession, for dealing, and for whatever else they care to think up." There had been a sting, going in; he hadn't been as fast as he would have liked. Ach, it was nothing – a cut along the ball of the thumb. Bleeding as a hand will; he sucked it. Shit, he's got blood on his trousers.

"You're a nasty little man. If there weren't black beetles you'd starve." The pain in the gut was disagreeable: he had enough of all this. He only had a paper handkerchief to wrap inside his hand. He felt under the counter till he found the lock release, walked out, dodged across the road and threw the weaponry in the river. Perhaps that was a mistake; hell with it, the police could fish the rubbish out if they should feel inclined. He hadn't been all that clever but he didn't care. He walked along the road to where he had left the Porsche, drove home, put a bit of sticking-plaster on his hand. This pain was getting worse.

Bad enough, indeed, that he decided to give the doctor a ring. Fellow went Mm, and Perhaps you'd better come in and see me, and maybe we'd better get you into hospital, and it might be a good idea if we got a few tests done. This was an unappetizing prospect. He rang Raymond's office number, got Silvia, without too many magic passwords got Ray, who was matter-of-factly brief.

"Nix hospital. *Salve me ab ora leonis*" a good sort of incantation. "Lie on the sofa. Go to bed if you want to. Unwind and breathe deeply. Nice long Brückner symphony on the player and I'll be around to get you organized. Unimportant, don't give it any thought."

When he pulled up his shirt for Dr Valdez' fingertips the pain went away: nice, these petty miracles.

"What did I tell you? Largely psychological, you've been putting yourself under strain. Got to get you cared for. Variety of kind women. Biddy to do the housekeeping, pigsty around here. Green tea and a few special things to eat. Feet up awhile, rest and stop pelting about, a day or so. Masseuse for an hour, I know a good one, she'll come here, smells delicious. A few more things I'll see to. Drift on a cloud of euphoria. For now, small injection," ticking the needle with his fingernail to get the bubble out. "Stretch out and be comfortable."

"What's that, morphia?"

"Heavens no, calming potion. Bath would be a good idea, lovely big one you've got here. What's this with the thumb?"

"Aimed to cut my wrists but got fainthearted," feeling a lot better and pleased at finding a joke. "You'll be back, Ray, will you?"

"Got to go to Paris so not this evening. Tomorrow yes. Nice to be rich. What you need is a few servants, as in grand hotel. I hope this woman's a good cook; I better go and dig her out. Just think of the food you'd be getting in hospital!"

Part Three

Barbour. Doctor Barbour. What is this doctorate? Not, it's thought, medicine. Literature, music? Law is likeliest. An alumnus of somewhere quite grand; Amhurst or Dartmouth. Jokes, and suppositions, have never brought one much further: PermRep he remains. Dr Smethwyck Barbour; would his friends call him Bill? Cronies, in the State Department, are said to call him Smithy. The sheen upon him is of privilege, power, old money. He's probably S.B.III or even IV. Eleanor his wife calls him 'Dear' in public, speaks of him as 'the Chief' and it's not seriously supposed she says Woofums in bed. There are no children known of.

A nice old house has been acquired for him, and pretty grand; spacious is the word for the reception rooms; suitable. Quite nicely furnished; Eleanor frequents antique dealers and has been known to buy pieces. There's a garden, there are offices, and there are a couple of aides and a secretary, ensconced. It's smooth here, and it's cool. Quite as grand as the Secretary-General and a lot more formal.

He is known to dislike and possibly to despise Strasbourg, but perhaps he also looks down on Brussels: it doesn't do to let those people at the Commission think one is at their beck and call. A nice striker of balances, he has a little plane and pops across a lot, up to Bonn (annoyed at the move to Berlin), over to Paris, to München (a lot more congenial). He has plenty of seniority, and even more discretion. Most of these people are heavy-handed, let you know they stand here for the Superpower. He can't abide the French but mustn't let it show. Brits are no better – sly, selfish and secretive.

To be truly discreet is a difficulty. Government's man in a sensitive listening post – these little towns are all eyes and ears; Bonn no better, or Brussels either. But neither is Washington his ideal.

This total conviction, that everyone bar ourselves is unspeakable, isn't of course confined to Washington.

There are diplomatic jokes on the subject. Often given the shape of a question-answer sequence.

'What is the difference between God and the French?'

'God does not believe himself to be French.'

'How would this apply to Brits?'

'They used to be quite keen on God. Sufficient unto themselves, no need of God nowadays.'

'So what about Poles?'

'They hardly need God, since the Virgin will always get them out of trouble.'

'And Italians?'

'God can be relied upon to be patriotic when really needed.' Some indeed were sceptical of this 'caricatural presentation' of Dr Barbour.

"I'm not believing this; he can't be that awful."

One can only describe people the way one sees and hears them. Or of them, mostly, which is going to be a bit spiteful. The Marquis, who being Foreign Minister knew everybody, said he was going to fix the little plane; wouldn't gather quite enough speed and crash at the end of the runway, goodness how sad.

Discretion is a state of mind. Dr Barbour had known Congressmen, and even Senators, lamed and sometimes permanently, by indiscretions. Avoid even the appearance of – but the bow cannot stay forever bent. He plays bridge, in quite a competitive way. Likes a spot of tennis but it's only doubles these days. A little night-music, sometimes.

Mrs Barbour, dear Eleanor, knows how to behave in public; runs the house well, good with servants, caterers, 'the help'. Hardly a satisfactory helpmeet. He has thought of a divorce, but her relatives are influential, could damage a career heading, if all goes well, for Undersecretaryship. He has been too long out here in the backwoods.

He had heard of Madame Bénédicte's discreet ways. No prostitutes; quite so. She had introduced Crystal; now there was a nice girl. He had to admit that he had formed an attachment. Warmth; exactly what was missing in his life.

He had not liked a facile expression, but – getting under his skin; how else would one put it? He wanted to feel that she was a private, an exclusive possession. He had been upset, to say the least, to learn that this was not so. Silly girl, had also 'formed an attachment'.

He knew nothing of the man; what he could learn he did not like. Bohemian sort of man, happy-go-lucky type, which somehow made matters worse. What could be done about this? Who could he take into confidence? Not, of course, any of his own people. The realization, disagreeable, that Madame B. was already in his confidence put him out further.

The man worked in some research institute, was said even to be a doctor. Could he be discredited, compromised? This was not enough. Means had to be found for detaching Crystal from this undesirable friendship: she'd got much too familiar with the fellow.

Oddly enough, Dr Barbour disliked violence, much as Dr Valdez does; they have that much in common.

He went in the end, making the best of a bad job, to Madame Bénédicte in search of a suggestion. What he learned there ended by reassuring him.

Intimidation. Familiar word, quite frequent in the mouth, without, perhaps, one's having explored the full extent of its meaning. Sarcasms, the cutting phrase. In debate a skill he makes use of; the suggestion that an opponent is ill-prepared, ill-briefed; his assumptions are laughable, opinions untenable, his grasp of the subject pitiable. The word has an intellectual cast. Even as a schoolboy (a tall, robust schoolboy) it would never have occurred to him to say, Give me that desirable object or I'll beat you up. In early years he had discovered the power of the snub, the glacial put-down. Physical intimidation, the large fist, the nailed boot, had never entered his world. Madame Bénédicte had a different viewpoint. One would not wish to enquire into where – or how – learned.

"You need know nothing about it. For payment made, value received."

"I don't want Crystal hurt."

"No no. That will be quite unnecessary. She'll get the message."

It had indeed been impeccable, in the sense of quiet, professional, anonymous, efficient. But there had been a sequel. This was disquieting, because it threatened indiscretions.

He had not been given the name of 'Monsieur Philippe'. Thought had shown him that his own way wouldn't do. An innuendo campaign – charlatans, drug addicts – could too easily be traced. The direct – the physical approach: nobody would think of him. Out of character.

Raymond had had an abrupt phone call.

"Doctor Valdez, I have to tell you that Monsieur le Marquis died." Yes, Patricia was the secretary's name. "This was sudden. It was peaceful. In bed, perhaps asleep, we can't be sure."

"I don't think he'd want any comments."

"There'll be an announcement this evening. It's not known yet. I'm ringing a few people I thought should hear."

"Like William? I'll save you the trouble."

"That would be kind. The funeral, you know – pomp and circumstance." And on top of this – William himself.

"Ray? Sorry to bother you. I'm not feeling too chipper. Rather a lot of pain."

"Ah? All right, loosen up, don't take any pills and I'll be with you soon's I get the car out."

So goes the world.

"Now – once we've got you comfortable – I want you letting go of everything. Exercise in complete quiet, with everything done for you – grand-hotel style.'

It hadn't been difficult to organize. Just the one detail at the end, while getting the man to sleep – writing a prescription for the nurse – telling where to find the door keys: yes, the Marquis.

"Poor old boy," said William. "I owed him a lot." And after a moment "High time, I suppose. He'd outlived his world. So nineteenth century. But I loved him."

"I know."

"I wonder" – the injection was taking hold – "whether there was a woman in bed with him: I shouldn't be surprised."

"Not the sort of detail they'll make public."

He had still one call to make.

"Joséphine? – Ray Valdez."

"I suppose you've heard the news."

"Yes, but it has only precipitated me."

"That sounds ominous."

"You free this evening?"

"What can you be implying? Whoever was in bed with the old boy it wasn't me."

"No such imputation nor insinuation."

"I see. An ulterior motive. Shall we be funereal together?"

"That's the idea. I can catch the evening shuttle."

"We going out or staying in? Pick me up here."

"On wings."

Thoughts on the plane were brief and simple. A moment of sleep would do him good, for it had been a busy day. Just the one though and that quite good theology.

Nothing gets wasted.

A lovely little kip, that. Ringing Joséphine's doorbell mightily refreshed. She was in a training-suit, as though just in from a basketball game.

"I can be changed in five minutes. You appear quite informal yourself," glancing at his little shoulder-bag.

"I left in a hurry. Evening dress is at the cleaners."

"There now. And I sent my crinoline to have the waist taken in. Well then – we've time for a beer."

"If you'll allow me to take a shower I do have a clean shirt."

"What's with all this mad haste? You're never thinking of going back tonight."

"No, tomorrow. I've also a toothbrush."

"So where are you thinking of spending the night?"

"With you of course, what a silly question." There, he'd got it said. He was grateful to her for making it easy.

"You're burning to be in bed with me?"

"Since the moment I laid eyes on you."

"Good, because I've been burning myself."

She wondered about this, between small sips, drinking out of the bottle like a boy. He choked suddenly, the giggle burning the inside of his nose. A Belgian beer, and its name is 'Sudden Death'. She watched gravely while he mopped streaming eyes and blew his nose.

"So this is serious."

"I'm afraid so," said Raymond. "I know only that I've been unserious for a longish time. I know the time has come for me to be very – very – serious." Since she couldn't possibly have known, pointing to the label on the beer bottle. She appreciated, with the shadow of a smile.

"The time has come to be very very brave – isn't that what they were supposed to say when they called you for the guillotine?"

"I would hardly need telling. They gave you, I believe, a clean shirt. With the collar ready to rip." You made, first your peace with God, but this thought he did not speak.

Her smile was getting broader.

"Speaking of clean shirts. . ." One had to stand up, however shaky the legs.

"Is your shower wide enough for two?"

"This is adultery."

"One reason for being very serious. There are more."

"I wished you to know only that I am also a serious woman."

"Let's dress and go out, don't you think? I've hunger pangs all over."

"I agree. While looking forward to being back."

"Oh just the neighbourhood pub. Because of all the Ministries round here, fairly quiet of an evening. But quite Smart. Not suggesting a place with green mould growing all over it."

Lots of old tat, rather dusty, at which Raymond looked with approval.

"That's why I brought you. Tourists look, and flee. At lunchtime it's full of Chefs de Cabinet, conspiring." The carte was in harmony, classic and antiquated. *Tête de veau en tortue*. Sweetbread with cray-fish. Grilled turbot on its bone.

"They've lovely fresh vegetables. And outstanding cheese. Not very romantic."

"I don't think we wanted to be all that romantic. Just a little." He stretched his hand across the table. She put hers in it.

"One thing I can tell you – that I won't be coming here again. Except with you.'" The wine was 'Les Bonnes Mares' of a year not ordinarily thought outstanding.

"Joséphine."

"I'm listening," wide awake.

"I have to be at work tomorrow."

"Which is today, and you're not looking forward to that ghastly plane."

"Nor to more of the same."

"No my poor ass, I'm coming with you." Doctor Valdez sat bolt upright in bed, heaving heard 'a funny noise'. "Ssh. Don't clutch me like that, you're hurting me. Geoffrey will not be pleased but will jolly well have to put a good face on it. That's my home you know. Were you frightened I would want to be your live-in shack job?"

"Let's get this clear," switching on the light to show he meant it, at which she gave way to the 'silent laugh' he is learning to enjoy. "I have no shackjob. It's perfectly true and I'll admit that there was one. She disappeared – some time ago. I didn't give her the sack, it's a complicated story which I didn't grasp then, don't understand now, and is certainly better left untold. I think she gave me the sack, but I've no idea why. Vanity to think I had anything to do with it. Like-liest is that she found a better man and didn't tell me; some idiotic idea of not wanting to hurt me." Whatever William's doings, about which he has some suspicions, he's not going to mention these to William's wife.

With whom I am in bed this witching three-in-the-morning. "Are there any cigarettes?"

"No. I stopped. It probably won't last long. I do these silly things." Now she was sitting up too, crying, shouting, wishing she had a cigarette, *Dio merda*, all at the same time. "And I'll be true to you for as long as you want me, filthy bastard that you are."

Old-fashioned novelists tended to clear their throat at such moments, perhaps with a coy disclaimer about the life of the emotions being too difficult for them: ripping aside curtains of intimacy, stuff like that. Jane Austen had the sense never to start. "You remind me of a phrase," said Joséphine, "which the Marquis used to quote; amused him. Something about Lowells talk only to Cabots and Cabots talk only to God? You're like that, really. You'll only be faithful to God in the long run."

He got up, slipping sideways not to disturb her sleep, walked into the living room, sat his bare skin on a chair, looked at the tall windows of the seventh arrondissement. Shutters were closed and doubtless booby-trapped (cat burglars have been known), a window hygienically open (the Sainte-Anne family brought up doubtless by an English nanny). There would be traffic still on the avenue but in these exclusive streets stillness. Rue de Grenelle, Rue St Dominique, Rue de l'Université. Palaces.

Stendhal had lodgings here, when he first came to Paris. In the house of the elder Monsieur Daru, who showed him so much kindness, spoke to him as 'Monsieur' and 'Mon Cousin' which nobody ever had before. But of him the old man said, 'the boy's barmy, or else he's a moron'. Ray feels much sympathy with both parties.

Moonlight comes in tall narrow streaks through the piercings of the shutters, falls crookedly upon a fine carpet. Moonlight of a similar sort but dirtier, less distinguished, had shone through his windows in Strasbourg. On the bare deal boards Janine had danced, naked, in slow, formal movements. They had watched an old gangster movie on late-night television, the young Jewish girl in the early years of the century in Brooklyn, who dances like that. Ray had found the music she dances to, on an old Artie Shaw record, the bottom register of the clarinet played slow. Very Emotional.

'Am–a–pol–a –
My pretty little pop–py –
My heart is wrapped around you –'

It wasn't, but he hadn't known that. The illusion had been perfect
and he surrendered to it. Amapola, his little opium poppy. It hadn't
been long ago, and it seemed as far as from the Rue de Bellechasse to
Prohibition New York. He had never said a proper goodbye to her.
Now he had to make a formal declaration of his gratitude for her
kindness. Goodness also. False little bitch she might have been but
he preferred to remember her as good.

He had got quite chilled before sliding back in with a warm, sleeping Joséphine.

Ruthlessly – she would be ruthless in large things too – she called
him very early. "To be at work," uncompromising. "I've got you
booked on the early shuttle. You've time for coffee." She was
showered, dressed, had been out for bread. . . Not 'packed'.

"I'm not going on that awful plane. And you never know who's
on it. It won't do to be seen together there. The Jesuit, plus mistress.
I have my little car. I'll drive down. You'll see me this evening.
Some palaver, with that fool Geoffrey." There is no mention of
William. "Have I your home number?" A kiss, a kiss amazing in
beauty.

The concierge was mopping the marble floor of the hallway, looked
keenly at him. A polite Good Morning. She'd known him again. Out
into Paris, his favourite, sparkling early-morning Paris, the workers
hosing down the roads, whistling. No sour-faced men and women
yet, trudging into Ministries, a quick *'petit noir'* first in the corner
café to give courage for the grind, a quick glance at the headlines.
Whizz on to the train with him, whizz past the Invalides, glance at his
watch, compare with clock, yes, he'd make it, he travels fastest who
travels alone. There'd be people going to early Mass in Sainte
Clotilde. Businessmen lurching on to the plane, all still asleep.

Silvia was apologetic in a cagy way, not sure she hadn't made a
muddle.

"I got on to something called the English Speaking Community. A Mrs Merryweather, isn't that a nice name, she was helpful and understanding. Long and short" hastily "there's a woman here now to see you."

"I'm broad awake," said Dr Valdez peaceably. "Good morning, won't you please sit down. Have you any idea what all this is about?"

"Thank you, er, not very. Mrs, er, Frau Bontempi said you wanted somebody to read aloud. I don't know why they thought of me except I used to be an actress. Er, Mrs Grey but call me Dolores."

"That's quite right. Er –" it was catching – "Dolores, this is for a patient of mine, uh, a therapeutic act, the thing is to know whether you are free, an hour a day, say the afternoons, have you got a car?"

"Oh yes, quite free, you mean husband, children? Yes I've a car – you mean it's some way out?"

"All right, let me explain, I want this man during that time to enter an entirely different world. That of Jane Austen. We'll pay you of course, exactly like a nurse."

"That shouldn't be too difficult. Sounds rather fun. He speaks English I suppose? Oh well, Jane's vocabulary isn't all that difficult, she's rather modern. I think I get the point, I hope I'm not too stupid for that. Which one should it be, to start with?"

"I'm not all that familiar with them; suppose you choose."

"Perhaps *Emma*, it's full of gaiety, is that the right word?"

"We'll take it as settled. Here's the address. I'll drop in the first time, not to interfere of course but just in case of any difficulty. You put him on a long chair, feet up, tell him to shut his eyes and unwind, you're the psychoanalyst in fact, the rest is up to you."

"Oh I don't think I'll be alarmed."

"Good, you leave your phone number and whatever with my lovely Frau Bontempi and tell her your best time, she'll coordinate."

"I think I'll enjoy it, it could be useful."

"I'm counting on you," said Raymond, with the winning smile.

He walked in softly; the door was on the latch. She'd found it all right; little Opel parked outside. But he only had to follow the voice, in afternoon stillness. A nice speaking voice, he thought, clear and matter-of-fact; not actressy mannerisms. They'd only just started, some preliminary explanation no doubt. He sat down quietly. William, sprawled on the sofa, didn't even notice. Good. She sat sensibly, upright, her legs crossed and the book on her lap; reading glasses. She noticed, but only fluttered eyelashes to show she had seen him. Her voice stayed level.

"'These were the disadvantages which threatened alloy to her many enjoyments.'"

"What's alloy?" There had plainly been an agreement that he would interrupt only if necessary.

"Literally a metal which you mix with gold or silver. Here, I think, to mix in the sense of lessening, diluting."

"Good. Sorry." William did not again interrupt until – 'having been a valetudinarian all his life'. . ."

"A valley- what?"

"Somebody old who fusses a great deal about his own health. Listen – 'without activity of mind or body, he was a much older man in ways than in years' – okay?" She went on smoothly to the end of the chapter. "'Depend upon it, a man of six or seven-and-twenty can take care of himself.' I think that'll do for the first time, I don't want to tire you."

"Thank you, I'm fine," sitting up. "Hallo Ray, are you there? I rather like your experiment. Mr Woodhouse is splendid. Knightley sounds pompous – okay, I didn't frequent the Marquis all that time without meeting more of these people."

"Oh good," said Dolores. "The English isn't hard – bound to say, you speak it well."

"Bright lad, our William," agreed Raymond. "I seem to recall that Mr Elton is the most frightful shit."

"Hush," said Dolores reprovingly, "you'll spoil it".

"I look forward", William, polite, "To knowing what happens."

"Oh good. I'll pop off then."

"Have some tea. Green tea!"

"Thank you but I've got to pick up a child from school." Diplomacy all round.

"I'd rather Jane to green tea."

"You'll get accustomed to both and addicted in a week. Woman make a good job of your dinner?"

"Marky used to quote Stendhal. 'Spinach and Saint-Simon have been my mainstay.' A couple more goes with your massage woman and I'll be a permanent sex-maniac."

"Perfect," said Raymond, abrim with self-congratulation.

About a fortnight later they were in Radiology together, where William has gone for a control. Dr Valdez has borrowed a consulting room and has a row of prints pinned up on the viewing screen, wheeling the Professor's chair about and enjoying himself, pleased because "Can't speak of a real regression but she agrees that in technical terms these are looking good".

"I'm certainly feeling less daunted," agreed William. "Mr Woodhouse likes 'a nice basin of gruel' late at night. Ol' Dolores is a bit vague about this – some sort of porridge? Let me recommend you a very small soft-boiled egg. I don't think it could disagree with you. I'm getting exactly like this."

"How astonished they'd all have been at a machine which sees through you."

"Or that tunnel which booms and mutters at one, saying there's an enemy submarine out there somewhere. Jane seems to have lived through the whole of the war paying no attention to it whatever. So sensible, really. But they aren't at all far from London."

"I suppose not," said Raymond who can't really remember." You know, all this is doing you a lot of good."

"Yes, I'm beginning to take an interest. Thinking of doing some work on the garden. Getting quite addicted to Jane. I mean Harriet Smith's girlish confusion over who she's in love with, it couldn't be more boring but I don't fall asleep, I still want to know what happens next."

"Because it's real. The world we live in, all the noise that's made about it is profoundly unreal, we look and we say ok, what the hell. The ethical problems are the same; who one's going to marry, is he the right social level and has he enough money. The man in the Kipling story says 'They're all on the make in a quiet way.' We're no different."

"I'm getting more energy. Don't have much pain either."

"We'll slack off on a few things and keep on with others." Knowing the Crab's little tricks, one's not going to make any foolish prognostics. That – as Raymond does recall – got Emma Woodhouse into a good deal of trouble. False hopes will lead to sad humiliations.

Monsieur Philippe had every reason – well, nearly every reason – to feel pretty satisfied about affairs. Business is looking up; there's lots of money about. That dodgy strong-arm operation, he hadn't liked that, and he'd got panicked into saying and doing foolish things, but there'd been no real fall-out. Threats had been made but he was pretty sure they were bluff: he reckoned he knew bluff when he saw it. Large part of his own stock in trade.

His man at arms, whom he'd picked for the job of bashing that doctor. . . no trouble there. Long-distance truck-driver who did a bit (more than a bit) of contraband; he had plenty of leverage on the fellow, and let him know it: he'd keep his mouth shut. Like all such folk, the more money they made the more they were thirsty for. The payment had been right, neither too much nor too little. The Doctor had been well and truly intimidated; gone to hospital and (one had got to hear) undergone a nice bit of facial surgery. They'd got the message all right; girl well choked-off; an efficient piece of work.

Everybody's been paid. The Principal (one wasn't supposed to know but he did) had jolly-well-coughed-up. Bénédicte would have told him straight that suchlike things are costly: good jewellery doesn't grow on trees. He himself had been paid, no messing: she's a good business woman. Cow would have taken a healthy commission. And so had he. Nothing wrong anywhere: there's a big difference between what the farmer gets for his cow and what you pay for meat in the shop. There are green pastures in that diplomatic world.

Still, there was a loose end, worrying like having a bad tooth and he'd need to have it out. He had to restore the balance, and better. One must never let people think they've got away with it. Retribution isn't always swift but it has to come.

He had to stay clear of the girl – Mireille, Janine, whatever she's called; she is Not discreet. While old mother Bénédicte who is very discreet had told him to stay out of her sight. From the lassie-Iñez he's got a garbled tale of a man – Parisian-sounding man – who had strolled around and scared the knickers off Mireille, in all respects fitting the description of the bastard who'd strolled so cheekily into his own shop. Who was this man? Had that little bitch given him away?

He'd only the one pointer to guide him; the connection with that doctor.

Now if that bad man came from Paris the chances of identifying him were thin. He was there himself quite often, and has a widish circle of acquaintance, but – on the other hand the bad man had shown – no? – a measure of familiarity with the town here. Checking on the doctor's ways would be a great expense. He is spending his own money! But if there's something to be learned. . . One is forced to the conclusion that he isn't spending enough of it.

Following the doctor's movements is both easy and difficult. Easy because this is an absent-minded man, whose eyes are unobservant; he drives about (going to work mostly he bicycles) without looking. Difficult because Monsieur Philippe has to use his own car, which is not obtrusive nor even conspicuous, but a good car is necessary to his own position in the world, and his is a Saab; one doesn't see all that many of them. If it were to pop up frequently in the field of vision even an absentminded man will notice. He had to ration his shadowings.

But then there was a piece of luck: there generally is, if one perseveres, and in a cause this good Philippe is patient. A woman came, to that dump in the old-town where no one came. Rather a striking-looking woman. And familiar with the dump; she had a key to the house and was toting a shopping-bag. When she came out suddenly, and climbed in to an open car with the top down – easy to follow – he obeyed an impulse. She led him a long way, out of the town; he was getting discouraged when. . . A village, up towards the foothills of the wine country – but she went straight through, turned at the top and in at the gate of a manor house, a 'château', quite a grand one, and here too her manner showed a familiarity with the place. One would make a few enquiries in the village. Oh yes: Sainte-Anne;

he knows the name. There was a Baron de Sainte-Anne, an occa-
sional customer (not a good one, for small pieces of jewellery: cheap
sort of fellow (for someone with plenty of money). He went into the
village baker; one could always use a cake or something. Did the
'thought-I-saw-someone-I-knew'; bakers' wives are all gossips.
Sure, that's Miss Josie. Uh? The Honourable Alexandra if you
prefer. Oh yes, of course.

A garage man. Saab might need a bit of tuning; d'you think the
plugs need changing? No, I've plenty of time. One can gossip even
better in a village garage – they've always time to chat. The thing
about worms is they keep on worming, and shift quite large stones.

Sure thing; Miss Josie'd been away a good while, in Paris yes,
come home – been in to have the car serviced. She married but it
didn't take; some fellow, know him by sight but one doesn't see him
here, lives in a house away yonder up the other end of the vines. That
was something, house built specially, must have cost a packet and she
never wanted to live there. Thought so, these plugs are the trouble
all right. Nice woman, Miss Josie, always a smile and a word. Not at
all stuck-up. Good tip, too. But the man there, typical Parisian,
country people aren't too keen on those folk, give themselves too
many airs. Nobody knew much about him; kept to himself. Got a
Porsche; won't see that brought in here for a tune!

Now that seemed worth following up.

Monsieur Philippe felt wary about the woman; she looked too
sharp. Carting rather fast in the little car; baronial disregard for
speed limits. One would take a look, but definitely, at the house 'up
yonder': found with some difficulty. Isolated too, one couldn't hang
about up here. Nice house all right. Very much barred and barri-
caded; that would be the loneliness, off the beaten track. Somebody
lived there – car outside. Little Opel, a woman's car. There might be
a Porsche and it might be in that underground garage. This façade
hadn't any face, told him nothing and better not hang about. Stick to
the other end, see if the woman turned up again.

She did, oh yes, and this is lovely – she stayed the night. Better,
and it got better still, because the Doctor dragged his car out (likely

to try and get into someone else's dirty old VW, wondering why his key doesn't fit), so he risked following that, and where d'you think it led him? Curiouser and curiouser. This would build into something and he'd have to think about it. Can't stay in ambush on this damn path which doesn't lead anywhere.

A nice thing about Joséphine; she doesn't ask silly questions. Especially not that one about are you happy? Ray whose life is the asking of questions also avoids this one. One knows the answer; there isn't any, and if there were, one would prefer not to know it. Like that other, of who hit him on the nose and why? William had wanted to ask that, and it hadn't done any good. Something to do with Janine's disappearance: let her worry about it.

Happier than before? Happier than he ought to be? About as happy as one ever can be; look, one just gets on with living, okay? There isn't any vaccine against misery. Nobody can slip a needle under your skin and there now, you're immunized. The Research Institute thinks about the physical world. We don't hunt madly for new antibiotics, or old pals staph and strep showing themselves so naughtily immune to all those in current use. Other people do that. We get a bit metaphysical about living and dying. Sure. Violence, or getting married, or the tango – all of them metaphysical subjects.

Joséphine complains about the flat. Yes, it is squalid.

He's not getting away with that! A tirade develops; this awful building is due to be knocked down anyhow. Move before somebody demolishes it over your head. Nasty little spaces. That electric wiring is a perfect menace. Suddenly the fast ball.

"That revolting alleyway is dangerous. You could just as easily have lost your life."

"Po po po. Old stories, long forgotten." She just looks at him, more devastating than words. As though she knew all about it. Perhaps she does. Perhaps she has talked to William; he wouldn't know. She hasn't said so (and neither has William) but she doesn't pretend that William doesn't exist.

"I might get a cancer. So might you!"

"And then we do whatever we find possible," said Ray peaceably.

She is not one for beautiful phrases, for the garden of lovely thoughts: she finds these in the births-and-deaths column of *Le Monde*.

"It's all right to die on the street when not on purpose – who said that?"

"Stendhal. He did too." She is still worrying about him.

Joséphine loves eating. After laughing heartily at his antique gas stove she has taken with enthusiasm to cooking on it.

"Well made. They didn't cut corners then, look at the thickness of this metal. And properly designed."

"Yes but one can't get spare parts any more, so that when it wears out, which it will. . ." she has got reconciled to Arab ways. 'Modern equipment' would mean a new set of cables, a new meter. The electricity company would have a fit. There'll be a ghastly fire one of these days.

"This living as though you were poor is pure hypocrisy."

"I suppose it is, yes." She never has been poor. But she loves his spaghetti; introduces variations of her own. There's this advantage to living in the old town; the little shops (where Arabs go) which have fresh vegetables, proper fruit. Supermarket once a week, a suburban couple pushing the trolley, ferrying large packets up the stairs. The butcher is a mortification.

"But surely you knew about that from before?"

"True. Geoffrey has a man in the country, trained to hang meat." She has moved in, is now used to the oddities – the pull-and-let-go in the lavatory.

She held up a round of bread with a bite out of it, took another and said, "Look, a map of France", with her mouth full.

"Very bad manners," said Raymond austerely.

"Yes, we did this as children. That's Bretagne. German bread, good for our teeth. Got tremendously beaten."

"For bad manners?" Hers are terrible. . .

"Of course. But still more, because bread is a symbol. The greatest there is. The body of Christ. You ought to know that."

"I do. . . It's the same in Poland."

"We must never cut bread, once it was sliced. Break it before buttering – and if we dropped it, get down and ask forgiveness." Taking another large bite … "Look – Pyrenées."

Yes. This is 'the upper classes'. She has never made any other reference to his 'being a Jesuit'. Adultery is for the poor. Arabs have scruples about it. Are very strict about it. Exact blood for it.

'Aristocracy.' He had noticed these habits in the Marquis. Amazingly scrupulous in all sorts of small ways, and no manners at all. Utterly ruthless.

William to be sure had lived with the old man for many years.

Raymond now understands William better.

William's grand life-style has been lowered, but the reader's maintained: as Raymond remarked, 'We'd never get that past the Social Security office anyhow'. Dolores herself said she likes to finish what she began. Admits to enjoying herself.

"It's totally different to reading it by oneself."

This peaceful countryside, which she doesn't even describe. The social fabric – of which she says nothing. Mr Knightley has farms and works at them, but where does the Woodhouse money come from? Are they landowners? Never a word about the ordinary people, who must have been bitterly poor. You wonder about the price of food, about taxes, oh, all the things that we worry about. Never mentioned, any more than war, or Napoleon, or the world outside.

"That's the point," said William, serious. "It seems deathly dull, and then I'm drawn in, and it becomes exciting and I'm listening with all my nerve-ends."

"But why?" asked Dolores. "I suppose because leaving all that out she concentrates one upon the real essentials."

"Which are what?" asked Raymond. Wasn't this exactly what he was after.

"Well, not just who loves who, and who's going to marry who." Dolores a little defensive, nervous of sounding ridiculous.

"Things everyone cared about. Miss Bates too, and the workers even if we never hear about them. Pride, and honour, and pain."

"Exactly."

"She wrote about what she knew. 'Let other pens dwell on guilt and misery.'"

It's a Valdez hobbyhorse. The world is like William, in total disharmony with itself. What the woman called the social fabric was more closely knit. They were in harmony with themselves and one another, and the land they lived on. They had friends. Look at today; nobody even knows their neighbour.

They died of course – but I'll make you a bet, not of cancers and not of heart diseases. In the cities of course, tuberculosis, typhus, dirt, malnutrition. Plague to be sure, since the rats were always with us; cholera. You notice nowadays that the plagues take a subtler form, attack the nervous system, where the immunity has broken down. Rather well suited to peoples who have forgotten their own purpose. Television, or the internet – these are plague-epidemics.

Ray's colleagues listen indulgently. You've got to remember, Valdez is a bloody Jesuit when all is said – sees God all over the shop.

"What did you think", William had asked, "about having your head bashed in?"

"I didn't think at all. Things like that can happen to anyone, and frequently do."

William is a great deal better. Proof, if you like, is that he's going to school to learn carpentry. Craftsmanship. As for the technical details, Dr Valdez takes no credit. Internal cancers have been known to stop, even to go away. The patient's own interior resources are the key. As for Jane – he's taken to reading them himself. Why shouldn't it work for me too?

Living with Joséphine has a good rich texture. Coarse now and then, gritty. She was eating Serrano ham on her bread and butter.

"What happens to the rest of the pig? Why can't we get Serrano sowbelly?"

"Have you ever read *Emma* which he is working at?"

"Of course I have; I was well brought up. Mr Woodhouse could never believe that anyone would think differently to himself.

My brother Geoffrey's exactly like that. But a kindhearted polite old man while Geoffrey is so conspicuously neither. That and the appalling vulgarity of Mrs Elton. This seems to be all I can remember."

"A searching analysis," lovingly.

"There's a great deal of irony," with just a small flash of lightning, "and a lot about elegance and delicacy. Soeur Marie-Thérèse came down heavily on both, since the great aim was to turn out well-bred girls even with nothing at all between their ears."

Joséphine has had a number of jobs. Doesn't believe in them much, unsurprisingly: the girls at that convent would have felt sorry for poor Jane Fairfax obliged to go out and earn her living as a governess. Well-bred young ladies – elegant – were sometimes persuaded into secretarial work for politicians. With a little seasoning, press attachée to a publishing house. Worlds which William got to know.

"Politics! Just the thing for crooks like Geoffrey." When young she'd wanted to be a sculptress, in rather a clean overall. After, that is, her National Velvet years. "The extremely severe discipline of a racing stable isn't that different to life among the holy nuns. Adolescent female sexual desires thoroughly well channelled." Or perhaps a poet. . . Not having a job is so much more elegant; didn't go much on up at seven and shaving clean at a quarter past. Working for Médecins-sans-frontières was all right – and of course unpaid; the paperwork is simply shocking. Being able to read and write is an advantage since so very few can.

A Jesuit education, thought Raymond, has its points: you progress from grammar to syntax, and long hours of the dirtiest work uncomplaining. Joséphine scrubs a floor as though her life depended on it.

As we were taught, mankind is different to beasts. At some point in development this was borne in upon us; that we laugh and can inhibit defecation. That we have a soul had also to be learned. (Poor George Orwell's lasting experience of the civil war in Spain was that his pathetically primitive boys walked out and had a shit absolutely anywhere.) History. . . he'd had a good professor, fond of really sadistic illustrations from the dreadful fourteenth century – 'that's yesterday'. The condition of the poor. Meanwhile, learning absolutely nothing from Crécy, Poitiers, nor even Agincourt the landowning aristocracy of France, with a vanity and imbecility you'd scarcely credit, got itself slaughtered. And serve it right. While the poor suffered, here is where you learn about the basic economy of the countryside, and how taxation pays for the rich. The rich! (warming to his theme). They are only to be stopped with a scythe to the hamstrings or a bellyful of buckshot.

Those knights – deserving all the man said of them – had very likely included forebears of Joséphine's. Had they learned anything at all in the few hundred years between? Vanity, disregarding all else, still characterizes their behaviour. The ruling caste, be it military (Dien Bien Phu was Crécy all over again), medical (the mandarinat; of elderly professors), bureaucratic or intellectual (never do anything simple when you can make it complicated) – all of it the utter ruin of an endlessly abused and plundered people of great worth and merit.

Not at all surprisingly Joséphine got cross and there was a huge blazing row. He learned something then which touched him. This woman who had been taught so much nonsense in childhood had also been taught a dogma. Never let the sun go down upon your anger. Like a child she came and said that she was sorry, and put her arms round him. "I was in the wrong and I know it."

Given a lesson, Raymond was ashamed of himself.

Dr Valdez is tired, edgy, ragged; short of ideas; no fun to be with. Needs a holiday.

"Yes indeed. We'll fly to Miami, preferably in the Concorde, and get carried by cruise liner to glamorous places in the tropics never before glimpsed." Especially in August.

Joséphine has been thinking.

"I might be able to borrow the Land Rover, Geoffrey is greatly taken up with his vines."

"Why do we want it?"

"Because there's no other good way of getting there. As children we rode but there are rough places where we had to get off and lead our horses." Recognizing that she has got it back to front –

"We have a cottage, officially a shooting lodge, high in the hills. I don't think anyone's been up there for years. The local forester, from time to time. It's highly ruritanian, earth closet and all. Nothing but trees for miles. Be fearfully musty, I shouldn't wonder. No electricity. But when the sun shines, which very often it doesn't. . ." Dr Valdez is an instant convert.

"I've had leisure to regret this. I packed enough for a bus load, had to throw half of it out. Geoffrey said I was insane, the fraidycat." Roads, increasingly potholed, led to a village – "there's a shop, there", gave way to woodcutters' tracks and the 'Maison Forestière'; the intoxicating Vosges smell which he has never experienced, of a stone-built house, a flagged kitchen and wood fires. The Verderer's wife, amused, gave them coffee, glasses of ferocious schnapps, a bunch of keys, adding ominously, "You can always telephone from here if anything goes amiss."

"The worst is to come," said Joséphine with relish. "The valley goes up steep. I hope I can find the way. . ." The track hereabout was overgrown with moss and the fluid mountain grass. Twice they had to pull aside broken trunks, rotted and fallen across. Obscure streams made for boggy patches. Quite large stones abounded. Until they reached a plateau and a space cleared for a cottage surprisingly large if only a log cabin of one storey.

"Stable," she said welcoming it as one does something long lost. "Haybarn, woodshed. Gamekeeper lived here in my grandfather's day. It'll be almighty damp so the first thing is to bring in logs." The housekeeper took command. The airing of mattresses, the punching at the kitchen stove, 'grille's a bit rusty', the opening of sticking windows. "I don't know what birds there are now but I hope there will be owls."

The well filled him with joy. The source underground filled a stone trough, lipped over a worn flag, lost itself in red sand. The water was cold, rich as a white wine, tasting of black earth, dead leaves.

Fire on the hearth burned well; old silvered beech logs. Mattresses steamed happily until he had to turn them. Then he could
open quite a nice Côtes de Nuits. Watch her cooking.

"Lara," he said after searching for the name. "She lives with
Doctor Thingummy in an isba with icicles all over it."

"I can only remember the tune, unspeakably sentimental. It was
in all the music boxes which used to play 'Für Elise'. I had one –
greatly cherished. What do you suppose they ate – Russian porridge?" There are two rings on the kitchen stove, and a little oven
below. The top is rusty, but will shine with a bit of emery paper. She
draws water to clean the table, hangs a kettle above the big fire on
the notched bar the French call '*la crémaillère*'. "For the washing-
up," sternly. "Your turn tomorrow." Romantic, is it? It's only risotto.
Of course there is no fridge, but there is a larder, delighting him,
with stone shelves and mosquito-wire on the window. A high
point was reached when she put a zinc tub of water on the stove, and
from the outhouse dragged in a hipbath. 'To this my father was
greatly addicted.' Romance centres upon Joséphine's shell-pink –
Aphrodite-pink – behind; lessens when he has the awkward job of
ferrying the damn thing out without spilling to be emptied in distant
bushes; mounts when he comes back puffing to find her in a long
white nightie wielding a hairbrush. It's an illustration from Dickens
– 'The lovely lady has her fortune told.' But the mattresses are dry
by now, and unexpectedly comfortable. He can be romantic then, if
a bit damped by 'Wait till you have to empty the earth closet and
you'll see how they grew wonderful vegetables here.'

Still, the morning was all he had hoped for, outdoing imagination
built upon 'You've never smelt an August dawn'. With this go two
astonishing visuals. One is the filigree silver magic woven by more
spiders than he knew existed. The other is the August harebell. That
there is also a light grey drizzle cannot bedraggle the spirit, cannot
alter nor dilute the flavour. Has he never before tasted the true juice?
Once or twice (since medical conferences are very insistent upon
creature-comforts) he has been handed a glass of 'good' champagne.
Far outdone as he has been assured by the stuff which costs a thousand francs a bottle. And outdoing that by just as far is the glass of

water kindly handed to him here by the Djinn. The difficulty with djinns is known: you can't get them back into the bottle.

Reaction set in around midmorning. He had explored the long neglected garden, in hopes of perhaps-a-few potatoes; maybe a vegetable marrow (hostile animals have left nothing for mere humans). One must also learn the patterns of grisly trenches where the shit-bucket is disposed of: Humus is more than composting dead leaves. A facetious American word attacks him; he is discombobulated. Depersonalized, dissassociated, decomposed. Like the compost which had gone to the making of the vegetable patch. Reality had disintegrated. He trails back to Joséphine who is peeling potatoes on the stoop: the rain has lifted and perhaps this afternoon there might be a glimpse of sun.

"I know," she says with the maturity he has not expected in a young woman: his experience is so small. "For a start, there'll be plenty of work. Any number of things forgotten which we'll have to go down the hill to find. There are no guns up here. The forester will lend you one, but we'll have to buy cartridges." He wasn't listening.

"Food for worms," he said. "Bury me in the compost heap. Bacteriological nuclear pile. Have me down to bones in no time at all."

"I know," she said again. "It's not romantic up here a bit. No sunset, no cascade, no blue lagoon. It's violent."

"It's good." He sat down beside her. "I'm glad you brought me here. I'm overtired and hadn't realized it."

"Sometimes in Paris I thought about this place. Where I had been happy." She dropped the last potato in the pot, threw the peeler in after it. "Sitting with friends at a café table. After being at the cinema, maybe. People who are secure and comfortable and who prate about violence. Namby-pamby and niminy-piminy. Idiots." He can feel thunder building up inside her. She wants to talk. "For years I. . . I knew nothing. I thought it was great. This is the life, this is where it's at, they know everything here. Sex all the time, sex all day, it got like it was something that walked around with you, sat at the table, applauded at pop concerts, you couldn't shake it off. I got so when I heard the word I went cold and clammy. Up till now." She turned and put her arms round him. "Thank God for you. Sex is you."

"Let's go for a walk while it's fine." Narrow shafts of sunlight came filtering through the trees, bundles of arrows hitting the bracken and the moss and the needle-fine clumps of mountain grass. "Comes on to rain we'll whip back to the cabin and make love and play cards and drink a lot of coffee."

She showed him how it had been well thought out, and cleverly made. They were at the very edge of a steep valley. That is the gully down which they throw dirty water. Along the flank of the hill is the path along which they had come, mounting to the plateau where the stumps had been cleared for the house and the garden. This was 'Camp Five', for above them the height rose steep and rough to the summit, looking so smooth and easy from a plane; fierce afoot. "We could climb it in mountain boots. I've only once been all the way up."

Animals, by the score. You'd want to go out early in the morning the way we did sometimes. I doubt there being any rabbits – fox would get them. Predators; pine marten, there was a polecat once, they like buildings. Lynx? "The forester tried, I think, but you know how peasants are, never happy till they've shot it." Hawks, wild cats.

"What do they prey on?"

"Mice, voles, shrews; they abound, or would if it weren't for the bloodthirsty. Deer the forester has to shoot to keep the numbers down. You might try for a few pigeons – think of pigeon pie. There isn't any live and let live up here. My grandfather claimed he'd seen blackcock, had fantasies about pheasants; I don't think that lasted long."

Yes: it didn't do, to upset the natural balance.

"There's a brutalist school in biology, popular with your friends in Paris, believes everything revolves round sex. Some of these people try to claim that the entire development of human behaviour is explainable by predatory sexual instinct. Rape is natural, justifiable, desirable."

"Oh yes, I've met a few of those."

"A depressingly simplistic viewpoint. The strongest and most successful genes, surviving and evolving from the stone age, are those of the most vigorous rapists. The whole structure of society is of no further interest. A sort of nihilism. You the woman make yourself attractive to be available to the biggest dick, which is the greediest dick, and help me first."

"It sounds familiar. I thought like this for a while. Do you want to try to get to the top?"

"No, I've blisters on my heels already; wait until these boots are properly broken in."

"Don't sit down there, that's an ants' nest."

"I wouldn't have got far, would I, in stone age circles? Get stamped out, pretty smartish."

"Gains ground, this theory."

"Sure it does. Natural resources are running short. Water. Topsoil. Good places to go on holiday – the unspoilt beaches. So grab. Brutalist logic – the successful grabbers are the rich."

"I like you the way you are."

"A shrinking minority. God. Civilization. Iphigenia. Antigone. They were due for the chop. So are we."

"What did Antigone do?"

"She went out at night to pay the last rites of religion to her dead brother, against the king's express order. He caught her and had her buried alive."

"She knew, and she did it."

"Yes. That is the Spirit."

"Would you?"

"I don't know, you see, and I'm very much afraid of being asked to find out."

This thin sandy ground dries out quickly, which is an advantage when walking home in one's socks.

"The Volk," she said, making coffee. "Give it a jig or a tale of bawdry and it's happy."

"You don't like it?"

"Mustn't hate it, or it would be *A la lanterne* with me, pretty quick. But I feel something pretty close to contempt. Harlotry is the only thing that sells. The rapists – yobs one and all."

"Yes, it isn't so much they're being unchristian that offends me but the Ignorance. No letters and no history, no art and no manners, and above all no humour – what am I getting Heated for?"

"Bernard of Clairvaux scourging the infidel," bringing him his cup. "You see? – you can laugh. We're on holiday. We love each other."

Yes, that's what worries him, but he keeps quiet about that.

"I keep thinking about pigeon pie," Joséphine went on. "I must have a word with the forester, see if he can get us some."

William's day begins, alone in this house built for more people, with green tea. This brew was like Jane; for some time you were unsure, before discovering that you couldn't do without it. Odd. His little teapot holds three cups (but two will do, the third's a bit stewed). Disconcerting is perhaps a good word.

His whole life, he couldn't start without three cups of coffee – the last after a shower, shaving – sliding over clean teeth.

One day in England, accompanying the Marquis on a call upon his opposite number there – Downing Street, an extraordinary rabbit-warren; we know about Number Ten but what are all the others – he had been peeled off by a deft soft-voiced secretary and given a taste of their amused hospitality together with tea; the 'real thing'. 'Milk and sugar?' they enquired blandly. 'The way you have it' – not to be outfoxed in diplomacy. Much merry laughter when he tasted it.

'Now picture yourself', said his charming host, 'crouched on some draughty airfield, in a flying-saucer helmet and a nest of sand-bags getting strafed by the Luftwaffe, they dug you out of the débris, handed you a mug of this and instantly you grew a new arm and a new leg. Inside there it's tinkle-tinkle with the Wedgwood and some-thing disgusting like Earl Grey but yours is the real thing – made by the police sergeant, you're a man now, my son.' Even the gentleman in question permitted himself a small superior smile.

"You're looking a whole lot better," said Bernadette. "Odd job mine," economically finishing a halfcup of stonecold coffee "see that written on a piece of paper, what do you make of it? Nothing at all. But Orally. . . a *whole* lot, a whole *lot*, or a whole lot *better*, Madame the judge might be let to draw three different conclusions, pity the poor woman, who knows that all three are lying."

"All three are telling the truth," said William.

"That's this dotty doctor of yours?"

"Haven't seen him for a while. Away, I think. Don't want any doctors." Even the massage sessions were down to twice a week. Only Dolores still, determined to get to the bottom of Emma Woodhouse (not long to go now). He doesn't know how to explain that. Uh, broadminded woman. Intelligent, experienced woman. A good and true friend. There'd be nobody he'd rather confide in. But dammit, a judge; nothing bleaker than a Judge of Instruction when it comes to that impenetrable maze and quicksand bog which is human behaviour. What words would one adopt? 'It's a very select society and you've got to be a Janeite in your heart or you won't have any success.' She'd think it was a Sect. Judges have a great distaste for sects, which are suspected of preaching subversion, of disobedience to the laws and the rules of the Republic. Bernadette isn't a candidate for the Janeites: he's not even sure he's one himself.

Police training, for one thing. Years in the Marquisate – yes and before that; the private lives of Ministers, and Presidents too, have little enough to do with the official face shown to the world, and their private thinking not very presentable on television either – have loosened and shaken a lot of shibboleths thought of as being as fixed in their orbits as the planets. But in the PJ, when you are a rising young man and they begin to think of picking you for the exacting training that will lead to special duties, they like to be sure that your thinking is sound. It isn't only medicals and workouts in the gym. There are the political indoctrination classes too. Total loyalty, absolute obedience. (William's conventions about thinking and doing have interested Ray Valdez.)

The Republic doesn't like sects. Dotty American groups – all claiming liberty of conscience, tax exemption. And the right to bear arms, under various articles of the Constitution embedded in jurisprudence and frequently upheld by the Supreme Court – are held up as horrible examples: we won't allow any of this in France. These fixed beliefs of ours go back to Jacobin tenets on which the Hexagon was built. Long before the Republic.

Police instructors lectured bored young men who had forgotten the history lessons they had yawned over at school. You go back before Louis Quatorze, yes even before Cardinal Richelieu, to the times when kings could scarcely call Paris their own, royal authority kicked about by Dukes of Burgundy, of Brittany, of Berry (places one can scarcely find on the map. . .) Piecing the Hexagon together had been a lengthy, difficult and blood-boltered affair and you had better believe it. Look at Corsica, will you – know how to find that on the map, do you? Nobody wants it and we can't get rid of it. Forever blowing themselves up – and us too, given half a chance. Independence my foot; can't you see that this would simply encourage more of those bastards in odd corners who steal explosives from quarries and don't want to speak French.

William's was a receptive ear; it all sank in and stayed there. It's only a step from there to people who put up a statue of the Guru ten metres high on the mountainside. From there, my friends, to Theosophists and Soroptimists and the whole gang of them. The slightest laxity and they've the bit between those long yellow teeth – preaching Civil Disobedience. The lesson you'll all learn, before tomorrow morning, is you don't give these people an inch.

Yes but the whole point about Janeites is that they couldn't care less about Corsica. He can't remember even the fussy ones, like Mr John Knightley who lives in London, as much as mentioning the name of Napoleon Bonaparte. Hell, they don't even mention the Duke of Wellington. Jane's people live their lives in this marvellous indifference to anything outside. Is that shocking or is it splendid? It's all inside him; he can't talk about it.

"I really wanted to ask Albert's advice about the garden."

"He's outside there now. Deep in thought about a vegetable marrow. You might ask him whether there are any beans left and if so to bring them in because I'd like them for lunch."

Turning things around in his mind, thought Bernadette. Whatever it is, doesn't want to talk about it. Nor am I going to push him. I'm not in the office now.

A woman, possibly. Our William (for she is very fond of him) wouldn't have any problems about Sex. If it were only that! Big tall old boy, not exactly 'good-looking' but definitely handsome. Riding around in that ridiculous Porsche; the girls would be falling over one another trying to climb into his pocket. There can't ever have been a shortage. Kept tight in a special compartment because of all those conscientious ideas about Duty: you couldn't get married there in the lifeguard brigade, it wasn't fair on the wife. Getting knocked over flat, there by the Honourable Alexandra (whom Bernadette has never met but knows a good deal about) – that was shocking bad luck. He'd had his years of great responsibility and unending strain, before marking time there with that extremely lordly Foreign-Minister, who obviously had great pull in the circles of the mighty, to keep anyone as senior as William.

This tale had been told her. William held officer rank, and life-guards of that calibre can look forward to a nice desk job; you won't have to punch a time card. The girl had plenty of money. Building that lovely house, William all set for a cosy sinecure, perhaps the Interpol office (no shortage of these grandiose institutions in Strasbourg and all of them basking in money, while a poor lousy investigating magistrate can't even get proper office equipment) – and the bitch walks out on him. In Madame Martin's book, the crimes listed in the Penal Code can each and everyone be attended by files-full of circumstance, explanatory if not extenuating, you don't seek to excuse but you do seek to balance. But this isn't penal: it's sure as hell in the Moral Code though. Bernadette Martin isn't a moral theologian, and glad of it. These are the structural, load-bearing foundations of society. 'This is something one just does not do. In this she can't find any matter for debate or discussion.' Albert can, or says he can. Very sorry but there are some things she cannot give way on.

From the kitchen window they are visible, heads together and deep in talk. There are things men mull over together – not all of them mechanical contrivances – and a woman 'putting her oar in' is seen as a source of confusion. Was that the source of this homely phrase? A woman does not row in the same rhythm. She hears a different drummer. Quite a few of Madame Martin's discussions with lawyers, prosecutors, tribunal-judges, meet with the same fundamental variance in standpoint. If she were ever to meet the Honourable Alexandra the girl would get given a piece of her mind.

Albert was deep in contemplation of the compost heap.

"Right, William, getting out into the garden, put a bit of colour in your face. Apart from being too pale you're looking fine, you know."

"It's about tackling the garden I want your views. Sick of looking at it. Want to make a start, but don't quite know how my energies will hold out."

"Be a job, all right. Single-handed, boo, even if in perfect health. That garden firm which did the original layout, why not get them to come and put it in shape? You could go on from there. Expensive, I realize."

"Yes. I was sort-of keeping that idea in reserve. In case it got too much. I was thinking, maybe that weedy jungle isn't as bad as it looks. Thought of asking perhaps would you come over, cast an eye, tell me what you made of it."

Foolish at the start, William thought himself; should he be saying from the start? The garden firm had offered a maintenance contract. Frank or Fred comes round every six months with a workman. Clean and refresh, prune and repair, spray against pests, sell him a few new goodies. He'd economized – foolishly – in the reaction after spending too much. And at that time he'd been wanting to do everything himself. On top of the world. The feeling of having won the Lotto, of the good life awaiting him. Joséphine saying she didn't want a baby 'just yet', making jokes about Victorian phrases like 'filling the nursery'. There was plenty of time.

The potty adventures, of former days. The conquests, idiot echo of the Marquis' way with girls: 'notorious philanderer' was another Victorian in-joke. The bargain-basement time; since they're that cheap have as many as you like. The trouble with that: one is so damn cheap oneself. Whatever one said (one said and thought plenty) about the 'Honourable Alexandra' – she was not cheap.

The Baroness, with her ladylike ways. That upright carriage, that clear-boned face. A – a – purity about it. Hardly the right word? No but the only one he had found.

Let's not get sentimental, laddy. He won't let himself think about it, now or ever. He'd made this huge mistake. No, she said, the mistake was hers – as though it were a cake that they could cut in half and share. She'd taken a ruthless path out of this mortal tangle. Married and not-married. He'd given in. Foolishly? This kind of thing happens, nobody knows why. People find it doesn't work, they get divorced. He doesn't like it, but if there's no other way. . .? Joséphine had simply refused, wouldn't speak of it.

The furthest she'd go had been 'I won't discuss it. I'll think about it in a year's time.' To that, better say nothing. Better do nothing? He'd taken that problem to the Marquis, who disconcertingly agreed with her. 'Reach for the lawyer, will you? The six-shooter is no way to handle a woman of that quality, you shoot yourself in the foot. Spend a great deal of money, gets you nowhere. Wait and see.'

He'd waited but all he'd seen was an upset stomach that went chronic and to which doctors, damn them, pinned a nasty name. So he'd given in his resignation, on all this, exactly the way he'd shoved the job; there's no going back.

What did he have left? This beeyoutiful house. She took nothing but the few oddments she's brought with her. No wedding presents, nowt. What about the house then? 'Treat it as yours.' Not nastily – nothing cutting or contemptuous: factual. He's never heard anything from Geoffrey; the two men had barely exchanged a word after she left. He never heard anything from the tax people. What did he have? A wife which was no wife. Himself, a man that is now a no-man.

Feel like having a girl? Not going to run to la mère Bénédicte. Who wants callgirls anyhow? Somewhere out there, he'd thought, he might get a second chance at living. Meanwhile what does he have? Emma Woodhouse!

What's that phrase which Ray Valdez likes to quote?

'Believe me, Brother, there's no one to touch Jane when you're in a tight place.'

What between the feeling better and ordinary curiosity – Ray's phone didn't answer. He'd tried the secretary at that Institute.

'Away,' she said indifferently. How long for? 'Sorry, don't know.'

Part Four

'The staff' sounds pretty grand; Dr Barbour speaks of 'my people' and every secretary is now a personal assistant: they speak of him and the word 'parano' is often used. These overblown expressions are a way of simplifying complicated structures. PermRep like all politicians lends himself to caricature but the reality is a bundle, complex and devious and tortuous, like most people. He's stiff with employees, talks about precision, exactitude. 'Don't ever use a phrase like round-about-midnight, he'll ask whether you mean ten to or a quarter past.' He runs a tight ship; is rigid, fussy, suspicious, authoritarian. Paranoid is a silly word because it's lazy.

Partly it would be his upbringing, and schooling. Fifty years ago he would have been given to Latin quotations, and still corrects the punctuation in written reports. Partly it's an inheritance of moral principles and political certainties. He has an annoying way of always being in-the-right, and rubbing-it-in. Being without humour is no help. Recently he seems to have been unusually tetchy. He hasn't been feeling very well, and hasn't made up his mind what to do about it.

It would be useful to consult a doctor but there are difficulties. He hadn't thought of it when last on leave and has at present no good reason nor even pretext for making the trip. In European medicine he has no great confidence; has heard of a good man in Heidelberg but there's a language problem. In England they speak English of a sort, but he doesn't like the fuss involved. To minimize the feeling that this is all too much ado he went to see a man locally, making the appointment himself. Dr Roger (whom he has met socially) is well thought of in the Community and there's no ice to break. A wide general-practice among the diplomatic crowd; an easy-smiling cheerful man and the great advantage is that he speaks English. He has a nice duplex in the Contades, is experienced with the Community's little ailments (epidemics of laryngitis. Carpal-tunnel Syndrome), makes little jokes, gives good parties, plays a lot of golf and tennis: small wonder that though his name is Pilkington he's always known as Blessington. But he's a careful man too, and serious.

Listens to PermRep, examines, writes prescriptions, would rather like a blood test. Dr Barbour jibs a bit at that; rather too public in his view (Eleanor can be sent to the pharmacy). Dr Roger understands diplomats; he's one himself. It is always good sense to have a second – a specialist – opinion. He suggests an eminent and excellent Professor in the Faculty. In this confidential consulting-room sphere his patient allows himself to pull a face; unenthusiastic. Dr Roger isn't a fool by any account. Man shares a widespread view; that the French are brilliant but unreliable.

"I do know a man, speaks excellent English, regarded as good if unconventional; does a lot in close harmony with colleagues in the States: suppose I were to give you a note for him?"

This would be comic but for Dr Barbour's obsession with never being indiscreet: the name Valdez means nothing to him. Crystal has spoken, too much and too often until she learned better, about her 'onetime' eccentric in the research institute. The name 'Ray' had been dropped, but not listened to. In community circles, for Strasbourg is a gossipy town, in this respect much like Bonn, Raymond's reputation begins to be known to a few people, such as Dr Roger, but hasn't reached the Permanent Representative, who allows himself to prefer a man in private practice to haughty specialists who speak a humiliating technical French and are arrogant, condescending. . .

Madame Bénédicte who never mentions a name if it can be avoided, and pretends not to know anyone's occupation, did not go into details. 'Young Mireille has been silly enough to form an emotional attachment.' The permanent representative of a Power has

weight in Community circles and draws a lot of water in her book. If
he expresses a violent dislike for anything within her sphere of activity, she does not ask whether this is rational behaviour; it so seldom
is. Something will be done, and he has the right to know nothing
about it: that's what he pays for. Success in business depends upon
getting other people to do the work for you. She wants a customer to
feel comfortable.

It isn't a coincidence either that Dr Valdez knows nothing about
PermRep; a scrap or two of Community hearsay – this isn't Brussels
but it's just as gossipy. Janine's demeanours, maybe misdemeanours
in the past had never interested him much: everyone has things in
their life they prefer not to talk about. She had floated into his and
at 'the bottom of his heart' (wherever that is) he had known that she
would float out. Such things are painful when they happen. William
had a notion that it was on her account someone took an acute dislike to his nose; a good job of surgery that had been – painful, very,
but pain is not a punishment handed out for sleeping with Janine.
You accept it. Pain is one of the world's basic realities. William is an
ex-security-guard and sees things under the bed. People use the
most brutal violence to man, as to tree, earth or water, for the basest
of motives. A man, a woman, a small child – such are the ways of the
Crab. There's nothing to say, beyond *Ad Majorem Dei Gloriam*, I beg
your pardon for the kitchen Latin.

"*Felix qui potuit*," said Raymond sententiously, putting Joséphine
instantly on her mettle. School Latin.

"Happy is he – I hope I may be allowed to say she – who can, perhaps could? – understand the causes of things. Rather a trite remark,
not? Who's that, Aristotle?"

"Henri Fabre, a very great saint. Marvellous writer, wonderful
scientist, the bastards in the Sorbonne wouldn't give him a job, he
spent his savings on a little cottage in Provence with a bare patch of
ground, made the greatest entomological study ever known and
while he was at it filled the garden with flowers and rare plants for
his beasts to feed on."

"You could do the same here." August is the month of many many sorts of spiders and the house is full of them, giving pleasure.

"A century ago Provence was not polluted. Somebody in England looked in a rockpool at low tide, said never again will man see what I now see. We're losing biological species a thousand a day. I can call spirits from the vast deep, though precious few of them will do as I say." It has been raining hard for several days and there isn't much to do but drink and talk.

Of the very essence of romanticism is the truth so often trivialized into cliché, that the adventure begun in sunlight ends in humid, chilly shadow. Marie has awakened the sleeping Manda in the field by the river by tickling him with a grassblade. He opens his eyes and her smiling face close to his own is haloed by the dazzle of the sunlight directly behind her. Jacques Becker's film is well known to both because *Casque d'Or* is a classic of the cinema and there is nothing in it that is not perfect, necessary: it walks the tightrope of talent stretched taut, flowers into miracle.

Those two have one weekend. As they come out of the dark little church where Marie has watched the comic, touching peasant marriage, the chill strikes her and she draws her shawl closer. Round the corner innocently wheeling his bicycle, is the traitor, and that evening, sitting on the doorstep of the little shack, Manda knows what he has to do, and that he has no choice in the matter. To die is nothing much but to renounce the easy path makes a man.

Neither Raymond nor Joséphine will speak of this. He has little experience of life, though much of death, but his instincts are fortified by the discipline he has chosen to follow, and – *allegro vivace* – to disregard. She in a shortish time has known something of the world, but a woman is born to understanding. The hair's breadth between pleasure and pain is her biology.

Nothing chillier than a chilly August. But the house is dry and warm; Ray has learned the art of a log fire. The last time down-the-hill Joséphine had bought beef, and to save this from going off had put it in a bowl with a bottle of wine poured over it. There are some bacon scraps, and one day they had picked a basket of mushrooms, so that she has made a bourguignon stew, which has been all night in the oven and now it smells heavenly: the biggest potatoes had been put in the woodashes, and a field salad made of 'the weed from the garden'. Here recollections of children's botany are better than his, since he has none at all. She has promised him ('is this mushroom an amanita?') that 'we won't die poisoned'. Another bottle, an extravagant one, Brother Gorenflot's favourite Romanée, is taking the air, not too close to the embers.

"'*Als ik kan*'" said Raymond watching the play of the little green and blue flames: "it was the motto of the painter Jan van Eyck." Joséphine has less trouble with Flamand (she is Alsacienne born) than with Latin.

"When I can? If I can? As long as I am able?"

"It has to be stronger than that, I think. 'To my limit'? 'To my last limit'. Or perhaps it is humble. 'Knowing my limit'."

"Ours is awful. 'We keep faith' – one wonders how often they did."

"I had the Van Eyck picture once, cut out and pasted up. Chancellor Rollin praying to the Madonna. In every line of him a frightful crook but his prayer is utterly sincere."

"Perhaps he says 'I will always be faithful to you darling in my fashion'."

"Yes, probably that's the best we can do," looking after her with love. "But you mustn't be cynical, my darling. 'To our utmost' and we make that ours."

"At school they went on no end about honour. There was an Irish girl called Honour. We used to tease her. She said it was quite a common name, there."

"Not a bad one, either. I had a book once of American history – Indians. *A Century of Dishonour* – one of the best titles I know."

Joséphine is remembering.

"There were things for which we had to give 'our word of honour' and one had to think carefully, before one did so. I don't have any left, I'm afraid."

"It is what we lose. It can also be what we win back." She stretched out her hand, and put it in his, as she had done in the restaurant, in Paris.

They've gone and modernized Gitanes! One of the last remaining symbols of la-belle-France. . . which should have been eternal, and a national monument like Guimard's Métro entrances. Joséphine's cigarette-packet was on the kitchen table; the petrol blue now a chaste Madonna colour, the neon-green lettering a slimmed and sobered white. The Gitana herself still danced the tarantella in her swirl of smoke, defiant as ever, but she seemed smaller, less robust; the famous black silhouette now a stage-lit sweetheart about to take a bow, as though knowing the performance is over. As a doctor Raymond is bound to disapprove of her but his affections remain intact. She is no pasty-faced Marianne smirking in the mayor's office but the France which always somehow survives, loathed by all and still inspiring love.

Joséphine came in upon the wool-gatherer from outer space, picked up the packet, put a cigarette in her mouth in a challenging way (she's not supposed to go over three a day but it was plainly his fault for standing staring) and said abruptly,

"How is William?"

"No means of knowing."

"Dammit, you're the doctor," snapping the lighter like the lock of a pistol.

"Quite right. He's a lot better. Beyond that, you may as well go to the casino, take a hand at blackjack. Give me a card, whoops it's a deuce, another, it's a trey, yay, one more I've got a five-and-under. Go for it and shit, it's a knave and I'm busted. A cancer can go coy, playing footsie, now you see me now you don't. Been known to turn back, don't like it here, I'm going on holiday. But one never can say, Right, you, you're paid off, goodbye."

(Just the odd time, a year turns into ten, the ten into twenty, fellow goes out on the street and is blown up by a bomb. The Crab had lost interest, went to play with a little girl of nine.)

Joséphine has listened to Doctor-Valdez-playing-cards; one couldn't for a moment guess whether she was interested.

"You remind me of Geoffrey saying 'he calls the knaves jacks, this peasant'. Oh well, I'm a very old-fashioned girl myself. There was one the other day – she's modern, you understand – got herself raped in an underground parking, said she wasn't at all bothered since her cunt *was* an underground parking. The more the merrier."

Raymond, straightfaced: "My dick when fully erect measures twenty-two centimetres." Joséphine has an acute sense of the ridiculous, bless her.

"My fan – the name of the rose is the Rose. Won't be rose-like without the help of Monsieur Saint-Laurent. Fresh sea water any good? The Aphrodite Anadyomene did no better." she sat down and started to peel potatoes. . . he could see her looking for a 'tactful formula'. They aren't any, but she tries to soothe – down, dog – her dreadful habit of being blunt. Can one put a thing like this on a rational footing?

"What's it like, being a Jesuit?" It is like, he thinks, the clerihew about a well known French philosopher.

> 'D'you know the creeda
> Jacques Derrida?
> There ain't no reada.
> There ain't no writa
> Eitha.'

"It's no different to being any other kind of man. Now and then it's exceptionally disciplined, like being in the Foreign Legion. Betimes they tell you do some weird things. One they sent to Seven Hills, that's somewhere near Adelaide. 'Make wine'. He didn't know a damn thing about it, makes now the best wine in Australia. But the Legion looks after its own you know, they have a home for the aged cripples. Meantime, can't you tell? I'm like the one in the Piaf song. You smell good of sea water, I smell good, of the Hot Sand." She bursts out laughing, lovingly.

"Mon Légionnaire. . ."

It went on raining, Phrases wore thin, wore out. Hung be the heavens with black gave way to never-seen-anything-like-it; the roof started to leak, so that one put buckets under drips, or one would have, if there were any buckets, and jokes about Sadie Thompson never had been that funny: when the battery of Joséphine's little radio failed, the Let's get the hell out of here became overmastering.

Down-the-hill might be a startling new inland lake but who knows? – maybe the sun is shining. Throw everything into the Land Rover and make a dash for it; nothing could be easier. What is going on in the world? This elemental violence appears excessive. Floods here and forest fires elsewhere. Tornados. The polar ice is melting. Krakatoa has erupted, very likely. Joséphine who is easily given to drama is working herself into a lather.

When violence gives way again to the humdrum, the banalities of being wise after the event appear in deepcut relief upon the frontal, still intact, of bombed temples. It could be something pompous about Look on my works ye mighty, but it's more likely to be 'I did tell you you were driving too fast.' Not that she'll admit it, or allow herself to believe it. She knows this path by heart. It's impossible to capsize a Land Rover anyhow. He did say 'Slow down'; at least, he always claimed he had.

Fifty years ago the woodcutters looked after the paths in the hills. They split logs lengthways and laid them diagonally, primitive but efficient drains; they cleared boulders from eroded slopes and packed them to reinforce soft shoulders. Some of these paths have been carved out wider, brutally, for the passage of today's heavy machinery: on others, no longer used, the housekeeping has been neglected. Heavy rain starts a hundred little springs and streams across the face of the mountain; torrential rain may be expected to start torrents, which wash the subsoil out into deep gullies. On the path down to the forester's house there was a kink which had originally been quite a long way from a steep slope, but over the years erosion brought it much closer. Quite large stones had tumbled into the valley; roots and stubs of long-ago trees had been uncovered, loosened, carried away in their turn. One would not notice, until the last minute, that what had seemed a big bank of moss and grass held together by a tangle of heather and bilberry was in fact a fraud; the topsoil had leaked away progressively because under it the sand layer had been carried off. This storm had sent the whole bank down a steep and nasty drop. Once the offside wheels of – even a Land Rover – go past the point of balance you are teetering on the edge of what will kill you very easily.

Sitting on the off side, which was beginning to sag slowly at first, but the momentum piles up, Raymond could get the door open but underneath him was a horrible yawning chasm.

"Jump girl – jump." No time for polite injunctions or pious ejaculations. Could be described as a bellow, a yap, a howl. He was ejected, in not even three syllables and what the Army used to call 'without vaseline'.

For Joséphine it was a lot more difficult, sitting on the near side. The door began facing upward; the driver's seat doesn't help matters; there are complications like steering-wheels, all sorts of fucking hazards. She's an athletic girl. Fear, which according to cliché lends wings, is more apt to paralyse, so she's lucky to be fearless. It took a very long time to scramble, and a bunch of muscles such as one doesn't think of using as a rule, and some luck. Donkeys are patient, obstinate, sturdy, tenacious. Brit virtues, these. The Land Rover was obstinate before tumbling, and that helped save her life, very likely.

She pulled herself clumsily to her feet: if camels are that awkward she's sorry for them too. Without any notion of speaking aloud she said, "I've probably sprained my wrist. Or my ankle. Or both." Oh shut up, ninny. Looked around in a drunken way. Oh God where is Ray? Limped to the edge, heart banging; this horrible slidy lip with water trickling over.

"Ray. God. Ray." She knelt down in the water and sicked up. Then she saw him, ten metres down, a rag, clinging.

He had slid, scorched, down hillsides on his arse and his elbow, but the several tons of hurtling metal had missed him. Perhaps it hit a rock; it must have bounced a bit. He was hanging on to a root, bramblebush or something. He waved arms and legs about; they seemed to work. He tried for a toehold. Under all this loose soil and scree there must be something solid. The distance back to the road was immense; also looking nastily smooth. Maybe one could sort of scrabble sideways. The ten metres of climb turned into thirty, of fearful work. Clothes sticking to him, what's left of them. Both the arse and elbow in a sad state but don't seem busted. When he got his face up over the edge he saw Joséphine kneeling there staring at him: she had followed every step from up above, too frightened to speak or even cry. They stood there tottery, holding on to one another. He said something silly. She began to laugh and cry and be sick, all together. Poor girl, she had nothing left to be sick with.

"Oh dear," wiping a wet dirty face on a wet dirty sleeve. "Geoffrey's good Land Rover!" Then she had to laugh again. That's shock, of course. "Thank you, Brits."

"What Brits?"

"If it had been Japanese I'm sure it would have gone over quicker."

"What do we do now?"

"We walk. Can't be all that far." Not too sure she could. Valdez is supposed to be a doctor. Useless in the circumstances.

"Don't think it's sprained, just a bad wrench."

"Perhaps it'll get easier as I go along."

It didn't take much over an hour: they were soaked through anyhow.

The forester made little of it. To hear him such things happened every day. Occasion for a good guffaw. Even his wife, dry clothes and hot coffee, aspirin, disinfectant, sticking plaster, was pretty unperturbed. Sepp'll drive you down to the hospital. Nothing very terrible, not as though a tree fell on you.

Good grief – townspeople would have been screaming for the helicopter. Sepp was even jaunty about the Land Rover. Ach what, we'll bring the hauler up, once we get the cable hitched on she'll wind back up nice as Nelly. Bring her down here for the insurance.

His own (Japanese) four by four was surprisingly warm and well padded. Outpatients were thorough but undramatic. Radios showed no bone damage. A tetanus shot would be no bad idea; that's a lot of skin missing off your backside, mate, but the rest is only cuts and bruises. Extensive, but there's nothing internal. You'll be pretty sore for a few days. Some delayed shock, the young lady, but she can go home if she feels up to it.

"Oh dear," said Silvia. "You've been in the wars again." Raymond's hateful colleagues were downright hilarious; a week's supply of jokes about Shortarse Valdez. He went gratefully to bed with some hot cocoa. There was a long but unanguished phone call from Joséphine. Geoffrey had screamed a bit but come round to a fairish level of equanimity. The insurance company will just jolly well stump-up. He'd been thinking of a new one anyhow.

Monsieur Philippe goes about his business but he seethes now and then; feelings of irritability that he wants to scratch. He had gone to a lot of trouble and it had sort of caved in on him. That pair, the doctor and the woman, whom he had counted on, seemed to have disappeared; gone on holiday very likely, it's the season for holidays, he'd like to get away himself. The man Barton was at home all right, glimpsed from afar a couple of times but caution, caution, it didn't do to be seen. He felt a standstill. He wanted to find some way of hitting the fellow direct, something that would hurt, damage.

He was reading the paper when the idea came to him. Simplicity and force, how had he never thought of that before? Some of these imbecile independence-warriors in Brittany had stolen industrial explosive from a quarry; dynamite, gelignite, whatever it's called. He knows nothing about the subject but it sounds quite simple. The stuff is easily placed without attracting attention, can be detonated at a comfortable distance. They'd blown up – at least, created a lot of damage – a tax office, a sub-prefecture. Symbols of authority to cock a snook at. Works very well. You create fear, uncertainty, apprehension, as well as the physical damage you cause. And you can be anonymous or not, exactly as you please. The more he thought about it the more he liked it. But how do you get hold of explosives? Not his field. .

The man-at-arms will know; sort of thing he does know. Monsieur Philippe is not keen on taking a lout like that into his confidence but has quite enough of a hold upon him to ensure that his mouth stays shut. A large noisy pub is easily found, where the company one keeps is unnoticed by anybody. Outline the notion after a few drinks.

"Explosives I wouldn't know. Sure I know how to do it, goes back a long way that, during the war, railways or whatever, stick of the whosit in the crankshaft. But that stuff's pretty closely guarded, sure, mines, quarries, demolition job on old buildings, but not sure

I can get you that. Be pretty pricy too. I got a better idea. Gas tank, ordinary butane cylinder, countryside's full of them, that'd be easy. Disadvantage though, weighs a bit and bulky, can't just put it in your pocket." Yes indeed. Open it, light it, you've plenty of time to get away.

"The price would be right."

"Mate, the price comes in two halves. Getting it, yes, I reckon that could be managed. I know of a village, up in the hills, the shop keeps them in the shed, haven't much more than a padlock to bust."

"No no, that makes it too obvious. But getting a key to fit this padlock. . ."

"Maybe. He might have twenty tanks there, the truck doesn't come round that often and one less might not be missed for a week or two. Would cost you though. But placing it, that's another ball game. No no, Nelly, there you're on your own."

"I daresay the principal might be expected to throw in a decent bonus."

"You tell him from me, pad his figure with a few zeroes, still won't give me the horn. I drive trucks, I have some nice stuff inside these trucks, pay my holidays in Bermuda, blowing up houses is too rich for my blood. Just for getting it – cash up front, and no credit cards. Liquid, mate, in the bank in Luxembourg."

The bargain was too steep, but Monsieur Philippe feels a raging thirst there's no quenching until that fancy palazzo goes up skywards.

All very well for him! – sparing a spiteful thought for Terry-the-Trucker, rolling in the profits from cigarettes, probably illegal immigrants, in fact you-name-it: muscles like Popeye and the brains of a black beetle. Monsieur Philippe is prudent. Stops the car a long way back: this hillside ground is dry and drains well but it won't do to leave any tell-tales behind. There's a bit of a slope down to the courtyard and just as well; carrying this gas tank is impossible. Brains are better than muscles. If the tank makes tracks that's unimportant; he is wearing an old wornout pair of canvas sneakers he'd found in the dustbin, and ancient gardening gloves. Thus equipped Minnie

Mouse crossed the courtyard with his burden. That was scary but he's pretty sure that bedrooms are at the back and nobody comes along the path which is a dead end and marked as such a long way back. Where to place his bomb? Not going to risk climbing steps – under the steps is surely best. The screw of the valve is hideously tight; he had to wrestle with that, sweating like a pig in a monsoon, what seemed a good five minutes. Once he had the thing lit, scramble all aircraft; he fair scuttled, backing the car till he could turn it, sweating, it's a Turkish bath inside, he's making enough noise to waken the entire village. He hears no bang but the whole idea is to be well out of the way before there's any bang. He was back out on the main road thinking of where to dump the shoes and the gloves before there was a distant whump, so unimportant one wondered whether that was It. And now there is traffic again so concentrate on driving rather slow and cautious. His mouth of course was cinder-dry and he'd thought of everything except water to drink.

"Well," said the gendarmerie brigadier, "you were lucky in a way. Pretty amateurish, if he'd known how to direct a charge like that in a confined space. . . not been getting on the wrong side of any Corsicans, have you?" William's friends in the PJ aren't greatly excited either.

"Impelled by vulgar curiosity," said Xavier. "Not exactly hot-footing it out there with the technical squad. Know better than to tread on the gendarmerie's toes. Of course, if the insurance people were to book a formal complaint, and if an investigating magistrate were to refer that to us, be a different pair of shoes. I can do a bit of discreet eavesdropping. What d'you make of this yourself? This your little pallywally or have you got some more funny friends?"

"I'm just an innocent householder," said William. "They've been very busy all morning collecting little bits of débris. A gas tank like this was stolen up in the hills and they may get somewhere with that. I know who and so do you, and where's the direct proof? Not perhaps a characteristic approach, which I suppose he thinks clever, and he must have an accomplice, like who punched Doctor Valdez in the eye, huh?"

"So patience; he's getting bolder; one of these days he'll trip and we've got him. I'll have a quiet collegial word with the gendarmerie lieutenant."

"Leaving me out of it."

This is the way it works, thought William. I surprise myself; I become indifferent to the petty ways of the world. The insurance man, chicanery personified, the explosives man from the City fire department – the man from the local paper (but Geoffrey is quite friendly with his editor; three or four lines in the country edition). Quite right; all this is so unimportant. I was a Janeite without knowing it. Knowing it, one enjoys it more.

He has been reading *Pee and Pee*, supplied by Dolores. Not at all like her reading aloud, but she has explained that.

Addicted he is; this one hooked him too, but 'not the same'. She's very funny but in a spiteful acid fashion he found himself liking less. Reminding him of the Marquis, to who indeed Mr Collins had been the bread-and-butter of Ministries, while Lady Catherine was a phenomenon one met with daily in the sixteenth arrondissement and around the Parc Monceau. Mr Darcy he had met with in many antechambers, while Mr Bennet was a well known and extremely cynical Academician who hadn't written anything in the last twenty years but made a very nice living for all that.

Dolores, appealed to, said that this was Jane when very young and alarmingly clever. He could agree that it was extremely brilliant but he didn't believe that Elizabeth Bennet would be so quick and so brave at answering-back. But never mind, said Dolores, this prepared you for the mature and beautiful Jane. *Persuasion* next and that is the best of all.

As he got further, yes; were they even so exaggeratedly ridiculous? Politicians' wives, every scrap as talkative as Miss Bates but far less kindhearted (indeed a great deal less sensible, and really quite as silly and as snobbish as Mrs Bennet.) Pillars of party-politics as vulgarly on-the-make as Mr Elton, especially with a Mrs Elton to push them. Worthies, as wearisomely in the right as Mr Knightley (to whom he had taken an instant and durable dislike.) And be honest, at the time when the Marquis had been a sought-after television personality,

interviewers had often been the Reverend Mr Collins in spades. He
had stood in the shadows, behind the lights of the 'plateau', unable
to believe his own eyes and ears. An excessively brilliant Minister,
dyed-in-the-wool National School of Administration, had turned
out gentle – and charitable – in private life, and that shed some light
upon Mr Darcy. In England as in France – or anywhere at all.

Joséphine was reading *Persuasion* which she said she'd found 'at
home', to the accompaniment of some doubt 'how it had got there'.
Her claim that Geoffrey had never opened a book in his life was certainly an exaggeration: the cliché of hard-riding claret-swilling
wooden-headed barons is one she likes to promote. Raymond's
acquaintance among barons is not large. He supposed there would
be more like the Marquis, immensely civilized, widely read; as many
no doubt with no great taste for the printed page. Given a guess he
would suppose that by and large a country gentleman living in an
ancestral château thinks of the library as an essential attribute of his
home even when he spends more of his time in the gunroom. At the
least there'd be collections of classics, calf bound, in the major European languages. Didn't the women read? Of course they did, and
does one have to say 'also'? All over north-eastern France you find
ruins, where the battlefields of '14–18 left quite often no stone
standing above ground of these country châteaux, just as, through-
out central Europe, you hear fearful stories of Russians burning all
the books to keep themselves warm; of drunken Americans wreak-
ing equal havoc: châteaux had also well-stocked cellars. Favoured
billets for the licentious conquerors. And under all régimes widespread pillaging was the rule. However, Joséphine's home has not
been attacked since the seventeenth century. You would have to go
back to 'Les Suédois' – in Alsace legendary figures of dread – to
find this sort of destruction. Both French and German troops were
generally kept in better order. It is true that the famous library of
Strasbourg burned during the siege of 1870; true too that the Kaiser
was horrified to hear of this, and ordered all the universities of
Germany to do what they could to make good Christendom's
appalling loss. One way or another there isn't anything extraordinary

about finding quite a nice little edition of Jane Austen – lacking to be sure modern critical apparatus and commentary by the likes of Dr Chapman – in the library of a European country baron. Some grandmother or great-aunt of Joséphine has left pressed country flowers between the pages as a bookmark.

She is enjoying *Persuasion* – now this is 'adult art'. Vague school-girl recollections of Mr Bennet being witty about that ludicrous Mr Collins had left no real mark. But Anne Elliot is nearly thirty. The bloom is off. In fact she is described as thin, nigh haggard, and slightly faded: now who does that remind Joséphine of?

Doctor Valdez is catching up on recent medical literature. The room, which is always full of books, lying about everywhere as well as in shelves up to the ceiling, has a pleasant literary feel of peace and quietude. Two people reading, and not much conversation to break a blessèd silence. In the silence, a small noise, definable as a chuckle.

"You're enjoying that. . . It was my friend Mr Kipling's favourite. . . I don't think I've ever read it."

"It was the last she wrote; seems generally acknowledged the best. There's a very dramatic Happening, as near as Jane will allow herself to get to *Violence*." Yes, Joséphine is also ripe to enter the Society of Janeites (playing a bigger role in Raymond's recent life than the Society of Jesus).

"What's that?" Bored anyhow with Americans being extremely earnest about diabetes.

"Stupid Louisa acting the goat, falls off the step of the pier, hits her silly nut and they all think she's DEAD."

"Like me tumbling into the ravine." Raymond is carrying a fine collection of half-healed cuts and bruises. "Good God. But she isn't. . ."

"Of course not. But makes I can tell you one hell of a stir."

We speak of a kindly silence. Generally, I think, we mean that our hearing is not – for a blessed moment – assaulted by the bawling of the world. There is another sort; the silence that obtains between two people in kindness with each other.

This was interrupted by Raymond yawning, at first imperceptibly but gathering momentum as is the way of yawns until it splits one.

"Is that a dog outside?" asked Joséphine, "or is the lighthouse sending fog signals?" It was nowhere near so late but

"One, two, three; Time, time."

It might have been three; far into the night; when the phone rang. Since Doctor Valdez is not in general practice this is a rarity. And probably a wrong number but he still has to get out of bed (having it next door one only encourages the thing).

"Yes, Valdez," and then he listened for a long time but Joséphine has woken, has even switched a light on. To help him listen? Or to watch his face. Sometimes it can be like a burglar alarm ringing in some office.

"You have to tell me, you know." He looks constrained, not to say embarrassed. He had said very little.

"You're not in any way hurt?. . . That will be my affair. . . I'll be along. Do nothing before then." He sighed and said, "I have to get dressed. Hazard of this business."

"I'm waiting."

"It was William. Someone seems to have put a bomb. No very great damage."

"Then what are you doing?" At that, a flash of sarcasm.

"I'm going to sit on the café terrace, drink Pernod and listen to the band." A Bogart line and rather a good one.

"Exactly," getting out of bed. "Order one for me." Ray looking for his shoes and wondering what to say. Whatever – it would be of no use.

Joséphine, equally, appears concentrated upon not getting her trousers on back to front.

"Darling there's no possible point. This may take me some time."

"I haven't bothered with a clean shirt. I'd better have a jacket, seems it might be chilly out."

One faces the music, as they say. Likewise, firing squads. Marshal Ney, it's said, took off his hat, said "Soldiers!" – hadn't time for more. Raymond has much too much time.

"I don't think this is the moment for discussion. Where are the car keys, bonjour?"

"There isn't going to be any discussion."

Now Leonora, facing Pizarro who had already raised the arm with the knife, says simply, 'I am his wife.' It's quite all right on the stage. That is what operas are for: to be dramatic. Nobody suggests that Leonora when dressed up as the executioner's assistant cuts an unconvincing figure. But why is Raymond's mind running upon midnight assassinations? Baron Scarpia turning to claim the reward of lechery, gets the knife straight up his midriff into the big nerve centre. 'Here is the kiss of Tosca.' Follows that heart-wrenching moment – the terrible line 'And all Rome trembled before you'. The candles on each side of the body; the prayer, kneeling, for a wicked man; the colossal slow exit. The curtain – we've had time for the pulse to come down into the low hundreds.

The Beetle is in no hurry to start. Battery rather flat; Wah-wah-wah in a nasty expiring-threatening way before lurching to life.

Leonora's line turns Pizarro to stone, cues that tremendous trumpet call. Hm, a lot of people have thought that a mistake. Big fluster – 'The Minister has arrived' – Pizarro yelling that he'd be there this very second – sad contrivances these. It should end upon those bleak monosyllables. 'I am his wife.'

Looking at 'the bombsite'; the house from across the courtyard; Raymond was horrified, stayed so until a long-buried comic memory restored his balance: William was all right and this really was not all that bad.

A harmless old gentleman had the habit of watercolour painting in the open air; set up his easel in the 'park': when there was a brief thunder shower the old boy scampered. After it cleared students gathered to discuss 'whether it was better art than before'.

The bits which had been dry – trees and stuff around the building portrayed – were merely blurry. But the architecture, fresh and still damp, had slid in peculiar ways. Trickled? Tumbled even; whole areas of window and masonry, slate and gutter, had disassembled. Dislimmed is the word. The result (which greatly pleased the students) was very much the sight which now met his eye.

"Superficial really. No very Great harm done."

Joséphine's eye, as it were dryer and less romantic, centred upon Dust. Homely household objects like the vacuum-cleaner. Dustbins full of broken glass. Dare one say it? hideously prosaic – dustpan-and-brush. Her concierge in Paris, a grey soul in a grey overall, fond of remarking what good friends she was with her broom. One didn't have to be Corsican to know that bombs are part of existence, really. A well-built house hadn't suffered – much – structurally. The essential is that William is unharmed, a bit unkempt but looking on the whole quite chipper.

William was standing there in a formal attitude of welcome, pale in a clean white shirt, upright, face expressionless.

"Not in any pain right now?"

"Not so's I notice. I might find a symptom or two in an hour's time." Joséphine, apparently, didn't find anything to say; stood looking about her as though she had been here before but couldn't remember when.

"The police have been?"

"They've only just left. That smell of cigars is our local gendarmerie, amiable and helpful as always. They'll be back in the morning, bustling about with measuring tapes and things, taking photographs. They aren't greatly impressed with my bomber, who seems incompetent. Mainly interested in where that gas tank came from."

"William, what the hell is all this about?"

"They think, and I agree, it was more to give me a fright than anything else."

"Revenge? For something you did?"

"Ray – remember me? Paid-up luminary of SPHP – sorry, acronym for the Service of Protection of High Personalities. That's largely a matter of being seen but not heard. Before that, some few years a working PJ officer. In either role, main preoccupation is to stay off the shit list. But in the Kripo you get heard as well as seen. You might have to arrest people, get confronted with them, maybe give evidence in front of a tribunal. They might go to prison. It's been known they feel a grievance, brood on it, have some idea of getting even when they come out. Which might be years later. D'you mind if we sit down? I'm beginning to feel tired."

And you're talking too much, thought Dr Valdez. That's all right, let him have his head, he's out of practice with violence, feels a scrap of delayed shock, he'll quieten down and then I'll take a peek at him.

"This is nothing. I'll get the police in the local office to look at it. My friend Bernadette Martin has sound advice on this theme – never make complaint. Just like a civil lawyer whose counsel is – if he's honest – never under any circumstances litigate. Working magistrate, she ought to know! Stay clear of what they call justice, and sit very loose to the world.

"You're a pretty good friend too, Ray. Came along with your Janeite stuff, I've learned a bit about that. Easier for me after years with the Marquis. He had a game too. Called it his Proust game, not that I ever read the stuff but listen to him and I know how Swann said the kitchen maid was like a Bellini picture. All the people he met with were like portraits in fiction. My role was to keep silent, listen, learn.

"'I had the Marquis to thank, too, for meeting you. You spun me this long tale, about the soldiers in the '14 war. Chances of survival extremely small, statistical likelihood of getting chopped pretty immediate. Me, only more so. So they played this game. Jane's world is the base for defiance, platform for enjoying their life minute by minute. I could see the point. Got this cancer, dodgy kind of thing, my age, pretty good way of looking at it. We were trained of course, your number can come up any time but that's mechanical, what's the doctor's word? – functional. You told me, the way to handle a cancer is in my mind. I got into this Janeite world.

"Sink right into that, one does; marvellous stuff. Thought myself observant, I had. See the funny side now, the way Marky did. All true, to our own time just as much. Cruel though, huh? – this perception of what our lives ought to be. Not much use at finding the words, am I? – no, never was. Codes, very sharp, exact definition, no ambiguity, no blurred outline.

"Know all about codes, learned a lot of them by heart, civil code, crimi code, code of procedure. Bernadette knows stacks more screeds of legislative juridical bullshit. Get tapped for the Protection

Service, code of behaviour, personal honour. What Jane calls delicacy, anticipate, respect for the man, he's everything, you're nothing,
his function in society. As a human being he might be worthless,
you're still bound, pay him his full due.

"Getting tired, I'd like a cup of coffee, don't want any goddam
green tea."

"I'll get it," said Joséphine. "I know where things are kept."

"Coffee, Ray, and cigars, all the things you told me to lay off. Shook
me a bit, this bastard with his bomb, for all that. Pain too, bugger it,
here we go again, bloody crab, tickle me up, never really letting go.
Thought of ringing you up, my old miracle worker, sorry about it
being middle of the fucking night, knew you wouldn't let me down."

Dying down, thought Dr Valdez. Quite soon, give him a push and
he'll fall over. Needs a good sleep and then we'll see. Remarkable
recuperation he has. Joséphine's cigarettes were on the table and
William reached over and took one. She brought a tray with three
cups, went back for the pot. Needs no telling, knows how much
sugar we take, how we like it.

"Thanks, Josie, exactly what I need. And hallo, where do you
spring from? Stupid remark; I know. You're living with my friend
Ray, very good idea, better man than I am. Didn't mind your living
in Paris. Screwing the Marquis, no harm in that, old swine but he
gave something too, all the women he ever slept with, I'm the one
who knows, right? I knew him better than anyone. The great enigma
false to all and everyone; to me also but he told me things he'd never
said to any living man or woman. I won't tell, that's my code, and he
trusted me. Keep faith with yourself.

"Didn't like your friends much, riffraff they were. You'll do better
with Ray. I like it too, you're coming to tell me. That's honourable.
Courage you always had.

"So here the three of us are, like a thing of La Fontaine, the miller
and his son, one of those. The husband, the wife, and the lover. Not
like something out of Jane. But are we all three the Janeites? We
ought to know, what to do, how to behave, how to be true, ourselves
and one another. We're three friends. Got to rely on each other,"
clanking the coffeecup heavily back in the saucer.

"You've made a hell of a long speech," said Joséphine quite tartly. "Better shut up now. Push you off into bed, but you better listen to me first. Make an effort. Won't take long." She was at once aware of sounding rough and impatient.

"Quite right, I'm your wife, this is my lover. Made you a promise, be true to you. Broke it. Lost my honour. That's what it's about – honour. You've understood it, it's not a game, Jane." Steadying her voice, making herself breathe slowly.

"Captain Wentworth served eight years for Anne Elliot, never saying, never complaining. All that time, she holds fast, she doesn't pity herself. She loves him and she allows herself to be over-persuaded, she's told that he's not good enough. Comic it all sounds, doesn't it? She's made a grave fault and she pays for it. Keeps her honour. Which I didn't, and you never reproached me. Thought yourself not good enough: there's your honour.

"While I played the whore. Until I met you," swinging her gun barrel to point at Ray. "I met you. Come to see me on account of him, he's ill, and what's the matter with me, then, that I don't stand true?

"God I'm hating this. . Need the biggest pastis ever known."

"I'll get it for you," said Raymond. "Have it."

"No. Do this cold turkey. Sure sound like one, look like one." Aiming her gun, the slow assassin, taking her time.

"God – I love you so. And to you I promised – when one is gone what's another's promise worth? The more I love you the more worthless I become. But if I've no honour left I must not destroy yours. I know you. Your promise was to God and you won't break that. You'll try to. You'll seem to. You'd tell yourself you'll leave everything to keep me. To keep you I'll steal, I'll whore, I'll kill. I have already – all that's left is to kill you; I'm on the way to that.

"So I must ask you to free me from my promise. Send me back where I belong. If he'll have me." Like a child ashamed of itself she had put her hands before her eyes.

"Have you?" said William, puzzled. "What's that mean, have you? You never went away. I can't give you away. You give yourself."

"The way I give you a cancer, yes?"

"Oh, as to that," said Raymond, "speaking as a doctor, I can't be sure of taking it away. You can, though. For love's sake, you can do anything." She looked at him steadily.

"It's because I love you, I do this."

"You are free," he said. "And with the blessing of God."

Into this unpleasantly charged silence Raymond brought something he has often been grateful for; isn't a sense of the ridiculous in horrible moments a precious gift? Joséphine has the consolation of crying and William is wondering where the next pain is going to come from and Doctor Valdez wishes to jump off the Pont Mirabeau into the Seine.

"I am reminded of the Greek girl who went to the theatre to see *Medea* and didn't like the tragic ending, so she said she'd write another, and instead of all the bloodshed they'd go for the day to the seaside."

In those enormous black cumulus clouds the fearsome build-up of electric current goes crack and discharges itself into the patient earth. Joséphine remembered that one can control oneself. One can stop crying. To hic and snuffle is below dignity. William regained the impassive face which is taught to the Protection Service in public at moments of anxiety such as when the President is shaking hands in a crowd.

"Might be a good idea," she said, "if we all had breakfast."

Part Five

And now on the road, rolling along, driving the Volkswagen towards home – 'home' is good – there isn't anything to be funny about here. Cringe, buddy-boy, because you are bloody well under the lash. Use all the clichés imaginable. It will be like Queen Victoria's Diary, a great many words underlined and a Plethora – there's a good word – of Capital Letters. He wanted to lie on the floor and howl; well you can't, not in traffic. In abject desolation it tends to take the form of literary allusions.

Like 'She loved thee, cruel Moor'. Rather too grand; he's not up to that. 'I have another sword within this chamber' – but not in the Beetle. You are smaller in scale. Play your little pan-pipe. That's more like it. Each man kills the thing he loves. This lasted some time, before he got another fragment of another quatrain. There is no chapel on the day on which they hang a man. It's Wilde, not bad either. Who has been abject and is now learning dignity. *Nota bene*, you are still stunned; the pain's nothing to what it'll be in an hour's time.

There in the flat are her clothes lying about – untidy girl. Her toothbrush hangs on the wall; last twist of the knife. *Persuasion* where she left it, by the bed. .

Or 'Give me a doctor, partridge-plump' – and that's Auden –
'Who with a twinkle in his eye
Will tell me that I've got to die' – something Doctor Valdez has had to do upon occasion. Thought quite good at it. Doctors are often sloppy in their accounting. Forget, and put things in their

pocket. Analgesics or whatever. There's probably some morphia hanging about here.

He won't you know. He is one of the Company; a bad one but we don't do that. Our training is that we don't give in to despair. There is also a simple exercise, about Sleep and his brother. When, as a boy, you laid-you-down, the Company discouraged sentiments about angels and good-night-sweet-prince. You were asked to recall that death is no different: Be ready.

He wonders if he is; he never has been. The flat smells of her. He has drunk too much coffee and is not likely to sleep. Sit in an armchair and read *Persuasion*.

He picked up the telephone.

"Silvia, I'm sorry, I won't be in this morning. No – I'm all right, just that I was up all night and don't propose to be disciplined. I beg your pardon for being troublesome, make excuses where apologies are called for. I'll be in this afternoon."

It seems a bit pathetic that of the three Janeites he – the initiator – should be the feeble-minded one. Well, it was time to find out for himself. 'Believe me, there's no one to touch Jane when you're in a hard place.'

Silvia, comfortable rounded woman, is better than competent. Very well, so she ought to be; she's highly paid. But so is he; what excuse has he for being this walking disaster?

"I have a number of cheques for you to endorse. If you'll kindly do that I can pay them in." She looks after bills, she has a little book for reminders, and she chases villains who pretend they'd forgotten. She'll be changing his nappy one of these fine days.

"I have to go and see the bank anyhow." There's an earnest man there forever wanting to 'build up a portfolio', who does not show vexation at Raymond's unbusinesslike behaviour but has a sorrowful way of conveying disapproval.

"Silvia, I'm thinking of changing flats."

"High time. You need a proper consulting room. People come here and are disconcerted. That reminds me, there's a man who refuses pointblank to come here. You have to see him at his home and this is tiresome too because he's paranoiac about discretion. An important diplomatic somebody, Head of Mission so please you, better wear your Sunday suit." The door has been opened to a general attack. "And you'll have to change that awful car. I can ring a few house agents, that should be relatively easy, you've pots of unused money and the bank will give great sighs of relief. And so shall I. But there's nothing I can do about your clothes. Or that car?" Crushingly.

"Next thing we'll be opening a branch in California." It is not really an adequate reply.

The grandest part of Strasbourg abuts on a pleasant public garden called the Orangery, laid out in the nineteenth century in the 'English' style of rustic-romantic then fashionable. At the far corner is the passably ugly and silly building housing the European Parliament, now crowded by newer, uglier and sillier buildings devoted to kindred bureaucracies. You can't go any further without tumbling into the canal, originally designed to join the Rhine to the Marne: over the bridge is the Robertsau.

This is just the diplomatic quarter, and in the large pompous villas lining the park are housed a good few of the Missions in which a lot of countries maintain representations to the Strasbourg Parliament together with the Court of Human Rights and a good deal of *und-so-weiter* (since much of all this in the public eye tends to read Blahblahblah.)

In the park is a pavilion with a terrace where the orange-trees are displayed, a lake with ducks walking round it and a halfhearted cascade: the focal point nowadays is an extremely grand and much starred restaurant where the diplomats come to eat, one suspects at our expense. The comic aspect of this is that it used to be a humble café in thatched-cottage style where one could drink a glass of wine under the trees: it is still called the Burehiesel which is Alsacien for Little-farmhouse, and speculators have made this into a snobbish watering-hole. The Orangerie is still a place where commoners with small children can walk around the lake, to the disgust of the ducks, but all about is a stifling feel of Holy Ground. Raymond Valdez, in his Sunday suit, wouldn't come here on the bicycle, leaves the Beetle a long way back. Here at night a security guard might easily shine a torch on you and ask what you think you're doing. The PermRep residence has a high gate, some nice trees lovingly kept, and a speak-your-business machine.

Everything was pitch dark but when he went through the move-ments the gate clicked, a porch light came on and electricity gave the front door just enough of a push to allow him into a marble-tiled hallway where a tall, erect, middle-aged man in slightly gruesome informal clothes looked him over carefully; carrying a doctor bag but doesn't look much like a doctor. Satisfied that he was, in a couple of quick question-and-answers, the tall man led the way past empty offices. "We'll go into my study." Here he turned on lights, invited Raymond to sit down, and began complicated explanations. Ray thought he had seen this man before – perhaps it was a photograph in some paper. The man sat at a big empty desk, shaded his forehead with his hand, did things to give himself more countenance. Man with the habit of command, but people talking to a doctor will slip into a simpler mode after a minute or two. Man complains of a number of odd ailments, which might or might not be linked: he has some papers too, and mentions Dr Roger Pilkington, with whom Raymond is acquainted. There was talk too of what his doctor 'at home' had said or thought when last consulted, which seemed some time ago.

One looks, mostly. One listens. One makes a few tactful remarks. 'That all sounds reasonable.' 'Perhaps we could have a little more light.' 'I'd like you to take your shirt off.' 'The divan there will do nicely.' And so forth.

"I think we can go some way towards clearing up these questions." One will rarely go further than that, first time off.

PermRep was also wondering whether he'd seen this man before, and if so where. Since he wants to keep all this matter as discreet as may be he doesn't make a lot of enquiry. Normally, before doing any business with anyone, he'd have his staff find out whatever there was to be known.

On, he would call it, the social level, he hardly needed listening posts. He stands here for the greatest power on earth; it's emblem-

atic and it's also very real. He can pick up an echo on anything that
interests him, have it put on the screen and read off. Hard to think
of an exception, outside this sensitive area: he doesn't want a word
anywhere which might start speculation that his health was worrying him. Vulnerable point; keep a close guard on that.

Dr Barbour is confident in his own eye, kept sharp by intelligence,
trained by experience. This man has unconventional approaches but
there's no scent of the charlatan about him. One or two good refer-
ences, without going into detail. A goodish professional manner. It
can do no harm to go a little further here. Man wants another set of
laboratory tests; well. . . At home he'd be hearing the same song.

The Permanent Representative – he's aware of the nickname; it
doesn't bother him – does not think of himself as arrogant or over-
bearing. It is his position, and that must be safeguarded. He cannot,
for instance, allow any breath of scandal. One needs some relaxation
from time to time. Nobody cares much about that here; degenerate
lot, the French. However, there are people here on mission from
most of the world's countries, and some governments are puritanical. Not to speak of one's own. A cathouse may be dressed up fancy,
remains the cathouse, but in Bonn he had heard a whisper about Mrs
Ben, a person said to be dependable: one paid of course the price for
that. Understands the meaning of the word tact, and an interview
can be arranged. He had been favourably impressed. A call-girl
string is one thing; a girl who simply needs a bit of help with the
garage and the phonebill is something else. Mireille, said Mrs Ben,
is a simple affectionate girl.

He'd have to say, got on comfortably enough with Mrs Ben. Apart
from that awful asphyxiating perfume so many elderly women are
given to. (A very well preserved sixty, that's hardly elderly; that's vir-
tually his own age.) He didn't like the name Mireille; too frenchified.
Have her 'rechristened' – word amused him in the context. Crystal
– she has an openness, yes, a transparency he found attractive.
Refreshing girl. With her, he didn't have to be wary all the time.

Something of an Idyll. He'd got really fond of her; had been in
fact taken aback to find himself. . . heated. Didn't quite know what
word was applicable. Possessive? Not 'jealous' surely? Irritable?

With a character like that one should never be surprised, surely, at her naïveté? She simply. . . hadn't really understood. She got quite cross, even. "But you don't own me, do you? You help me with a lot of expenses and I'm really grateful – I try to show you I'm grateful, too. I only want to be fair." He hadn't liked to admit even to himself that . . . hell, the damned girl has a boyfriend. Some riffraff chap, bohemian of sorts; she doesn't take kindly to any probing and he doesn't want her thinking she has any hold on him. He doesn't know who it is. Doesn't want to know. She's popping in and out there over-often; two or three times not-here-when-wanted. Well; she's not a sort of slave. He can't claim exclusivity. But she seems extremely placid about share and share about, and this is getting up his nose.

Cut her off? There, though, he's 'unwilling to admit'. He doesn't like thinking about it, because his thinking is far from clear. He just doesn't like it.

For sure it hadn't been clever to take this minor irritation to a har-ridan like Mrs Ben. A distinct relief to find the woman so profes-sional about it: so unsurprised. Like something on his skin, a growth of sorts he'd once had; unsightly, it worried him. 'What's that a sign of?'. The dermatologist had a thin, icy smile. 'Nothing at all.' A quick puff of anaesthetic spray, the smallest nick of the razor. 'There; you never even felt it.'

"We'll have her detached. It'll be quite simple. You need know nothing about it. It costs a little; there are people who will need pay-ment. Leave it to me. It's preferable that you stay out of whatever is decided. I'll bill you; that's all. You have there a perfect security."

"You propose a sort of intimidation?"

"My dear man – whatever I propose you're unaware of it."

One evening Crystal had been crying a good deal; red-eyed. Sign of upset, a sullenness. It's nothing. Girl's got her period. The next morning he was busy; 'reading the papers'. He combs through these, it's one of the jobs. Looking for little signs – upturn, downturn. Not so much 'economic'; Bonn have people for that. There are other ways of perceiving confidence, prosperity – or a certain slackening. His private line buzzed; something he had absolutely forbidden to Crystal.

"That was absolutely vile," a hysterical tone. "You have to promise me you had nothing to do with that." He could be freezing while
remaining perfectly sincere.

"I know nothing whatsoever about it. This is a private line."

"Have I your word of honour?" Idiotic remark, very French, that.

"I don't intend to repeat myself." Killing it, glancing across at his
secretary, who was assiduously marking a FAZ article. A Company
boy but pretty junior. There was no need of any remark. Once had
been enough, when the lad was posted to him.

'It's a comfortable little job. Undemanding except of an absolute
discretion. You understand that word? Bear in mind: a breath in
Bonn and you're counting those subversive penguins on Kerguelen
Island.'

The old woman had demanded an immoderate amount of money
but knew better than to ever mention the matter.

Raymond Valdez never had any notion at all that Janine moved in
diplomatic circles: it's not the sort of thing he was curious about.
She knew lots of people, had lots of friends. She is an artist. When
one works in that sort of business, and more still when one hunts
work, any acquaintance may turn out useful. She is warmhearted,
talkative, flirtatious – she has to be. She could be over-blatant. He
had known anger, even sudden rage. One couldn't expect a round-
the-clock humble devotion.

There is when one comes to think of it a well-known and perti-
nent parallel. The Marquis would have been reminded of this and
would have chuckled over it. Raymond has never bothered reading
Proust; takes too long and is too much trouble; no doubt one would,
if the circumstances were right; if sent, for example, to study the
penguin population on Kerguelen. William hasn't either; had no real
need to . . . since during the years with the Marquis extrapolations
had been fairly frequent. Robert de Saint Loup has a tiresome girlfriend somewhat like Janine; known always to Marcel as *'Rachel-
quand-du-Seigneur'* from her imagined resemblance to the girl in an
opera popular in those years. Marcel, jealous soul and can be catty,
can't stand her and is forever dropping nasty hints to Robert: gold-

digging little bitch and the world's worst actress into the bargain. Robert, upright and generous nobleman, won't hear a word against her. She is shy, timid, over-sensitive, and Marcel frightens her.

It isn't really a parallel but an approximation, of a sort frequent enough; men when comfortable with young mistress are indulgent (a row every so often livens things up), don't ask too many questions; comfort is secured by vanity. Rachel can be horribly spiteful – and so can Marcel – and are we any better?

There's no great harm in Janine; there's plenty in Madame Bénédicte.

Old Mother Riley had a daughter Kitty, but La Mère Béné as the police call her is mother to nothing but her own evil thoughts. She'll slip up one day and they'll get her. They aren't in fact in a great hurry: there will always be people like this, another might be still worse, and politically speaking, in these diplomatic circles nobody wants a noisy scandal, so don't rock the boat. She sells sea shells, says William's friend Xavier who is busy learning English.

The old woman doesn't blackmail people much, likes it to be believed that she could if she would; knows a great deal about turpi-tudes, including those of police officers and important municipal functionaries; keeps a firm grip on the girls, and also on a few people who do dirty jobs; she has plenty of leverage on 'Monsieur Philippe'. Since she never does anything herself she needs them, but they couldn't denounce her without exposing themselves to pursuits they prefer to avoid.

Rebellious girls, obstreperous girls, might often get a bit beaten up but no harm is to come to Mireille, harmless and at present the treasure of an important personage. Frightening her a bit won't come amiss; just knock off the boyfriend. Knock him off how? Bit of violence, mean to say? I don't want to know, that's no concern of mine, I only want her scared off. How you do it's your affair.

Monsieur Philippe doesn't go in himself for violence; not his thing. He's adept at weaving webs, but that will be complicated, will take time, will be expensive. It seems simpler to arrange that the boyfriend gets given a smack, and let the girl know obliquely that here's a thing happens when she's over-affectionate in the wrong direction. He knows a fellow to whom strong-arm comes pretty naturally at the best of times: Terry the Trucker is a strong-arm pin-head. He has plenty on that idiot, whose long hauler is mostly laced with contraband out of Istanbul.

He invested a bit of time and trouble; old-mother Benny is very hot on the expense account and he will have to justify every penny in looking up the boyfriend. An easy target; scientist chap, biologist in one of the Research Institutes, absentminded type, Professor Sunflower on a bicycle, lives bohemian-style in the city centre, scruffy place full of Arabs, down a handy narrow alley, this is pure jam. So easy in fact he doesn't bother learning any more. Terry gets told to lurk-in-the-shadows, give the bugger a black eye, and ticketyboo. Terry's heavy hand is pricy but he never asks questions. Mother-Benny never pays one; remembers you in her will, tells you what stock to buy, stuff like that. The Council-of-Europe people have plenty of ways of doing her big favours. She doesn't send in a bill. Some people want a taxfree Mercedes, others dabble in Corsican cows; others again import something, have it relabelled as of Community origin, sell it in Taiwan. Juice enough for all and a bit over for Monsieur Philippe.

Janine, an innocent girl, childishly so where her emotions were involved, learned – obliquely – that if you make a bit of money on the side, rather too easily, sooner or later the bill does get sent in.

Quite abruptly Dr Barbour asked, "What happened to your face?"

"Road accident," said Ray, hoping to make it sound more peaceable than it had been.

"Nasty things," conveying some disapproval; the French have far too many of them.

"Yes indeed. Superficial – looked worse than they are when half healed." Should have seen me when I got mugged in the alley, but he didn't say so. PermRep thought about it, and not wishing to sound aggressive added, "Could happen to anybody." A doctor might perfectly well refuse to see anyone before bruises healed.

"And did," sitting to write the jargon abbreviations for the lab tests he wanted.

"Worse things can happen," taking the piece of paper. "I'll be in touch." Raymond produced the Research Institute's card.

"Better early than late."

"Let me show you the way out," remembering his manners.

William is thinking. Why is there never time to think things out properly? Of Bernadette Martin's 'sound advice' – to do nothing. Of solitude. It was another of her remarks 'let fall'.

'*On est tout seul, tu sais.*' It covered the physical aloneness which he'd had time to get used to, here in this house. Joséphine was back? Really? She might suddenly disappear again? One would echo the great joyous shout of excitement and delight in the Jacques Brel song – '*Mathilde est revenu*' – the wonderful ending 'Since you are there, since you are there, since you are there. . .' The singer does not wish to enquire further, could not bear to think beyond this moment of now, and here.

It covered responsibility. What you do, you do alone, decide alone. Nobody else is to blame.

William thought, briefly, of his youth. Early days in the police. His brother whom he admired was already a soldier, doing well. They shared an idea, that service was honourable; you do something for your country, you volunteer, it's professional, you give of your best. Even then, he'd followed his own path. It had to be 'the best'. Me and Paris: the country boy frightened, feeling the challenge, welcoming it. That was all right; tall boy well set up, smart appearance, alert; it hadn't taken long for him to be picked for a team. He'd not been good, really, at team work – oh, he got on all right, the others accepted him but only just. They'd always felt some instinctive reservation. Kind of an apartheid. Something mocking in the camaraderie: ol'William thinks himself too good for us. His Commissaire thought him bright but didn't like him. That boy – I don't know, gets on my nerves somehow.

Better, in a Kripo service. They like them bright there, allow for a bit of eccentricity; you're more of an individual. Good marks for being dogged, conscientious, thorough. Tell that boy to do something you don't find him goofing off in a corner. Solitude – was it his enemy?

A bright, ambitious, vicious chief – himself young, pushing for higher rank; first in and last out; took a fancy to him – I like this boy, he's not sloppy.

Physically he'd been good; lots of fast, nice coordination, basketball. He'd thought of getting tapped for the Protection Service, liked the idea. When it came he didn't hesitate. Plenty of the colleagues said Fuck That. Our time off is bad enough; those poor bastards never have any time off at all. Sure it's more money, and it's a promotion, but shit, where's your private life? Can't call your soul your own, over there.

It seemed to him, he'd never had any proper private life, anyhow. He'd been brought up hard. He liked discipline. Five-thirty in the morning – out there with you. Here you were in perpetual training, the physical fitness is the first thing of all. He loved it; this was satisfaction. That smart appearance, properly polished shoes. He liked the lessons, was good at them. This is the boy for us.

On these teams, instant success. Back-up boy, point boy, bag boy (there are several purely technical angles to close protection). Put him on with a few difficult ones; the Chief Rabbi, the Spanish Ambassador, the Environment Minister (tricky; would the hunting crowd like to see him with egg on his face!). Hostile crowd meeting and election rallies; dockers and schoolteachers – and school children too, with highly imaginative ideas about covering the Minister in scarlet paint.

He'd become a star. *Chef d'Equipe*, and the man they all asked for. He'd reached the top of his profession; the man who walks behind the President. He'd understood the most important thing of all: the total discretion. Whatever you see, hear, sense, you know without knowing. Around the President, the turnover is pretty rapid as a rule; he'd stayed much longer than most. And when your Chief comes to think, from the confidential notes, the medical reports, that you are slowing or slackening even that microsecond, there are cosier berths. The Marquis had asked for him, got him. The old man had colossal pull (been in every senior ministry untold years, since de Gaulle's day). Kept him. He'd been happy; here he was happiest. You learned so much, here most of all. The high personalities of the

Republic gave astonishing amounts of confidence – he got to know the Marquis as nobody did, ever had. The old boy prized his reputation as the Great Enigma; didn't care what he said to William.

Oh well, he'd known everyone; the Pope and Citizen Kane: 'to bed with Marlene and to breakfast with the Kennedys'. At one of his parties William had first laid eyes on Joséphine; tall and elegant, not giving a damn; grey frock and very little jewellery. Gone head over ears; only the cliché will do, here. His job by then was to stand in the shadow, immobile unless something were to happen, watching. He had neglected his job, for the first time he could remember, because he couldn't take his eyes off her. She had known. Complex things happen in astonishingly simple fashion. William had been to bed with girls he had told himself he was 'in love with'. What's this word love? The most famous word in the language and what does it mean?

A cook asked a famous cook for a job. He'd prepared his answers to every possible question, brought along his CV carefully written out in every step. The great man asked only one question: '*Tu bandes pour ce métier?*' The translation is not as simple as it seems. 'You've a hard on for your trade?' But it means, 'Does your passion overmaster you?' To the exclusion of everything else? The boy said 'Yes' and got the job. An art; you don't think – you've no time – about anything outside.

Getting married? That's another complex affair and he couldn't remember anything about it but the Marquis insisting on being his witness, very beautifully dressed. He'd given them a pair of silver candlesticks, extremely fine, eighteenth century; William is looking at them. Joséphine didn't seem to have said much when asked.

'You're the vertical man. One doesn't meet with them often.' as though he were some kind of rare butterfly.

Resigning everything – he remembered that better, the Marquis saying, 'Can't have this, can we? – Joséphine married to the security man!' 'Benedick the married man' – who the hell was Benedick?

Well, one didn't lose just-like-that more than twelve years of the trade; seniority, experience, value; the job he knows and is good at. They never left you very long anyhow, you weren't allowed to get mouldy in the Protection Service, you'd get Napoleon quoted at you

– 'After thirty man loses the aptitude for war'. You remain a crim-brig officer with a good rank, diploma'd up to here and high-class confidential notes; most of us can look forward to staff jobs. You can go to commissaires-school, Saint Cyr au Mont d'Or just outside Lyon, you'll sail through that.

He went to see his chef, Place Beauvau, Ministry of the Interior – a man only a year or two older than himself.

"Married! Oh well – it happens. You're living in Paris? I've an instructor's job for you, out in Vincennes. You'd be good at that; I'd like you to take it. So you can, too. . . howsoever. . . The Marquis has been in." Damn him, what's he meddling with now? "The old man – as you know – still a great deal of pull in various quarters and I'll be frank with you, I don't want the old bastard being occult in my back. You've been with him a long time. He tells me that your wife. . ." He's not going to tell me that Joséphine has been manoeu-vring. . .? "No no no. But Strasbourg, it's not at the present open but it will be when the Schengen agreement. . . now that would be pretty good and you've the profile if we adjust a bit here or there; I'd sub-scribe to that one. Political, you've pretty good English. These Ger-mans in Frankfurt, you go in high up and you're answerable to the Premier Ministre. So you think about it and if you want to talk about it with your wife. . ." That was a nasty daggerthrust to take home with him.

They were living in the 'family' flat in the septième, Ministries all around one; he didn't like it at all. Joséphine didn't either.

Out by the Bois de Vincennes one could find a nice apartment – the twentieth arrondissement is a bit East End when you've been accus-tomed to the seventh, but it's not so much that as – Instructing is a very good job in police books; well paid, secure, easy hours. The 'cadets', boy and girl trainees for the Protection Service. He'd be good at it too, could grow to like it. He knew most of the colleagues, got on well with them; they had a pretty good life. But this police world, where conversation revolves around the television programme of the night before: can you seriously see Joséphine in this milieu?

He knew about her plans, for Strasbourg. Her brother-the-Baron was giving them some land and she had her house sketched out. The

job? – like all these political deals it was a lollipop, with some luscious perks. You aren't taking the tram to go to work there, my boy.
But whose pocket are you living in? His Ministerial years had taught
him a good deal about the politician's arts.

But he'd taken it, hadn't he! He'd asked the advice of friends; none
had hesitated. He didn't have a lot of women friends. Most of his girl-
adventures had run aground within a day or so, on the rocks of those
impossible hours: he just hadn't enough time for what they wanted.
He hadn't known anyone like Bernadette Martin then. He'd started
to compromise, and he wasn't good at that. It had been many months
later that he began to feel those odd twinges of pain. The two facts
might be linked but where was the evidence to support theories?

He had 'no family'. This was surely sentimentalism. A PJ. group
is quite fond of referring to itself as 'the family'. Or – absurd the
Marquis' household; that strangely tight-knit cluster, the world seen
from the kitchen of the marvellous house in the Rue de l'Université
– the cook and the secretary; driver, housemaid, and yes, even
'Madame de Maintenon'. We knew each other's birthdays and
bought flowers for them and Charlotte would have baked a cake.
Ridiculous? Bernadette Martin didn't think so. 'Oh yes, that's a
family.' Adding a remark William remembered. 'Without a family a
man trembles with the cold.' But the nucleus is a man and a woman,
isn't it? 'And why then, do you think, they should want so to have a
child?' This very morning he'd said as much to Joséphine.

"Are you going to give me a child? Of my own?" fiddling with the
temperature of the shower – she likes it a bit hotter than he does –
"I'm going to have a damn good try." Sentimental, is it? The woman
he had known well enough to raise the point were oddly biased in
favour of monogamy. One day over the coffee cups – 'You ever been
married, Charlotte?'

'Was once. Not any more. Buggered off, so he did. Oh well, learn
to do without. Not such a great drama as they'd have you believe.'
Or Patricia, a woman still young, fresh, attractive. Warm, a laugher,
you couldn't possibly call her a priss. A friend.

'You ever sleep with other men, do you, Lavigne? Have the odd
bit on the side?'

'People do sometimes very kindly offer.' And then, seriously –
'That's a terrible trap, you know. I've tottered on the brink, once or
twice. What would I say, to my children?' She has two little girls.
'Think of it as normal, what one hears,' he suggested.

'What you hear. What they hear too, yes. But that's not what they
know. Not what they expect from me, either.' Or Bernadette, judge
of instruction with twenty years' experience.

'Statistics are crap. You must know this, from your police years –
crime, from the misdemeanour right up to the Assize Court, begins
ninety-nine times in the hundred with a miserable story of a broken
marriage. Anything else they tell you is just so much toasted marsh-
mallow.'

Feminist talk. Women get very hot indeed under the collar. 'What
collar?' Ray Valdez would have asked. 'Are we talking about horses?'
They'll embark upon a tirade, talk your ear off; about the men going
off as cool as you like, shrugging and saying it wasn't important,
they'd had a few drinks, they'd been very tired at the time, no need
to make such a fuss, it's meaningless really. Not like the days when a
girl might get stuck with a baby. This, the women will say, is quite
typical. Men are exactly like a child who breaks a toy, says he never
meant to and it was no good anyhow. The woman will always be left
to carry the can.

William had asked Albert, on a stinking hot summer day which
had made Albert's gardening unusually intensive. 'You'd think I was
a stoker on the flaming *Titanic*.' Sitting with a quiet beer in the
arbour, down at the end where vines had been trained to go over the
top, and a rusty old table underneath.

'You ever commit adultery, Albert?' Wonderful line, Ray Valdez
would have called that. But beside friendship, and being in the shade
after burning sunlight, and that incomparable first shot of a cool
beer, this is a man who likes the direct, factual, concrete question,
answers it the same way.

'Yes. Not a good experience. Not recalled with any pride or satisfaction.'

'Bernadette know?'

'Women always get to find out.'

'What she do?'

'Did. Said. Nothing whatsoever. Left me stew in it. Plenty written on her face.' Took another long drink of beer. 'Not going to talk about it.'

No. That advice he'd had already, in bits and pieces at various times. Regarding Joséphine, say nothing, do nothing: it won't help.

Albert went off for a long blissful shower. Bernadette home from work, already showered, in shorts and a band round her hair, was making mayonnaise in the kitchen, invited him to stay to supper.

'I've made too much. Never mind, it'll keep.' The judge quite often talked about her work; it interested her that his professional background would often shed a bit of extra light, perhaps fortify her in a decision she had made but not yet pronounced, wanting still to 'think about it overnight'.

On this, but on many other occasions of the sort, he had got to know her mind; Albert's too, though by character he's a lot less articulate. This judge doesn't like cut'n'dried formulae, accepted wisdom, pat answers; is ready to go back and think again. Do we 'have a view' upon whatever? Sometimes. One might have come up against philosophic groundrock. But we know so little. Do we have a view, say, about divorce? Not really. It's one of our modern plagues: two hundred years ago we were more dogmatic. (Yes; as in Jane.) Only for the very rich then, who could afford to defy society. What d'you want to do – legislate against it? Like Americans with what they call liquor? It's bad so forbid it? Sure it's bad. It kills people, like the cholera, and we've not found the vaccine. Ravages; you've only to look at the children's faces.

'But just because adultery is a sought-after commodity on account of being fashionable, doesn't mean you have to invest in the shares.'

Yes, police work is just the same: the well-worn lecture gets delivered over and over; Sisyphus rolling his stone.

'Help me peel these,' shooting a pile of langoustines on the table, sadly clutching claws and pathetic little antennae.

'So you've got to try to get each and every individual to accept where the responsibility lies. Since there's no rule any more, no ukase from society, no brakes on the cart. Two in a marriage; if there's two to get behind the stone, does make the road a bit less steep. I'll push if you'll heave.' Albert came in still mopping at his wet hair.

'Sounds like something the bishop said to the actress. . . Ooh, langoustines, goody.'

'You shut up,' said Bernadette who was skinning tomatoes, 'or I'll plunge you in the boiling water.'

Monsieur le Baron, Joséphine was told, was in the gunroom. Joséphine likes the gunroom, albeit with a small shudder; in her childhood, when they had been really naughty, they got sent here to be beaten. It's very manor-house here: tall mahogany presses with fishing-rods and cute little drawers for flies and lures, which might be looked at but never played with. And a mahogany table, with Geoffrey and several guns, and the paraphernalia of pullthrough and soft flannel, and the wonderful intoxicating smell of gun oil. This is a religious rite; Geoffrey loves his guns. There are two rifles, the 'big' Mauser, guaranteed to stop a charging boar, and the 'little' Remington; the twelve-bore shotgun, an English-made side by side, a terrific treasure: his little one for blackbirds and thrushes, naughty greedy beasts which tear at the vines. Her own sixteen-bore must be here somewhere: bouh, it's a collection for John Wayne (Geoffrey has a Winchester-repeater for repelling boarders, Pancho Villa and the like). Roundabout is a lot of plumage showily mounted, cock-pheasants and things, now a bit dingy. He looked up and nodded, rubbing away at imaginary flecks of rust. She perched her bottom on the table and watched in silence.

"So you've gone back to your husband. . . Good. . ."

"Why is it good?"

"I don't know. . . Family counts for something." She knew that at the back of his mind was his own wife, Liliane, who is like her name, a thin pale blonde, alarmingly ladylike. Joséphine had never liked her much, had been heard to say that just as Geoffrey belonged in his gunroom, so Liliane belonged in 'the flower room' along the passage, where she keeps her gardening tools, always meticulously clean. But it's not her fault: she is childless and it's a great sorrow to them both.

"In this house," grunting and sighting down a barrel," we don't believe in divorce."

"Well don't point that thing at me; I don't either."

"Don't be silly. Inoffensive as a clock. As you know very well I only meant. . . in this house our family has lived a long time. We've obligations. Traditions."

"We've never done anything."

"Not much!" Nettled, glaring. Why is it that I'm always tempted into irritating him? "We've held fast and we've held our own." All set to launch into his history lesson, which is as well worn as Bernadette Martin's lecture on adultery. "Back in the old times we survived the Bishops – greedy pigs they were – the Emperor, the ghastly Duc de Bourgogne." Banging the table; he really means it. "Turenne. . . The Bourbons." The series of splendid engravings, showing the Joyous Entry of Louis XV into his good city of Strasbourg, hangs in the passage which is rather dark; they aren't in very good condition.

"The Revolution." Shucks; fleeing to Baden-Baden. "Bismarck. The Hohenzollerns. Finding ourselves German again."

"We bent with the wind."

"When I think of that unspeakable Hitler," wrathfully picking up another gun.

"Our father successfully claimed his heart was bad. Much surprise when he found that to be the truth."

"He was genuinely pleased to be flying the Tricolour again from the tower. Monstrous bonfire for the village. You and I weren't even born. I don't mind being French, myself, it doesn't seem to me all that important."

"They try to make it important. Remember the radioactive cloud when the power station blew up? It stopped dead in the exact middle of the Rhine because it didn't dare invade the territory of the Republic." Geoffrey didn't suppress a grin and it was unpompously that he said, "Being patriotic means being true to this house and this village."

He is proud of his vines. He inherited a lot of rubbish, now produces beautiful wine, some outstanding. The Rieslings have never been more than 'honest' but the two Pinots, the white and the grey, get recommended by the most snobbish of sommeliers. (She remembers with amusement that the Marquis had some in his cellar and produced them with a flourish; her 'password' to those elegant invitations.) Competing with the vineyard world is Geoffrey's life work. He is right to feel pride.

"I've just brought off rather a good deal with the Brits."

"Brits!" Joséphine does not carry the English next to her heart.

"With no doubt a lot of condescension on their part." Mimicking – "'To marry a foreigner is a sure sign of failure.'"

"I'm not marrying them; I only want to make them drunk."

They both laughed; they are 'friends again'.

"That imaginary superiority they cart about is their great handicap and they can't see it."

Pleased with her peace-treaty Joséphine moved on to the library next door, a place where Geoffrey never set foot. Their father, who neglected his vines ('good enough for the pubs in Strasbourg') had been an omnivorous reader and an enthusiastic book-collector. Joséphine likes this room, where Liliane never came either but where she as a teenager had spent hours of content. Papa's Anglophilia, so characteristic of French country gentlemen, meant wonderful things like *The Bridge of San Luis Rey*, or *Death comes for the Archbishop*. How disappointed she had been to be told that *The Story of San Michele* was all nonsense.

She feels she's had enough of Jane for the moment; wants something romantic – fruitier, more like a Gewurztraminer; lights on Robert Louis Stevenson (enjoyed in childhood, wasn't sure she'd recapture that now). *The Ebbtide* and *St Ives* and *Kidnapped*. Alan Breck the 'bonny fighter'; she'd played at that in the orchard. Took it down now, hesitant: the old binding opened on the last page.

'Whatever befell them, it was not dishonour, and whatever failed them, they were not found wanting to themselves.' A bonny cadence, a bonny writer.

Joséphine surprised herself by sitting down and having a cry.

Silvia thought Doctor Valdez looking still 'simply awful'. It is not her job to say so. She isn't anyhow the kind of secretary who supplies aspirins and Alka Seltzer for the hungover business men. Brisk, but the maternal is kept for her own family. Doctors are supposed to be able to look after themselves. This one can; highly disciplined. Compartmented; the 'Jesuit' stuff is not apparent. Here in the Research Institute they come all sorts. This one is sloppy, eccentric, forgetful; nearly always polite, generally kind, mostly considerate: anyhow he's a good doctor and she's proud of him. For a longish while now he's been dabbling in private practice and he could be building up something of a real reputation as a good man to consult. People ringing her up for appointments, it's impossible in a place like this. She disapproved greatly of that awful scruffy flat. One has to cut one's coat according to the tailor one can afford. She wants him in a proper suit and not as in that phrase of his – 'freshly deloused by the Salvation Army'. A consultant must go to a good shop and be seen to be wearing money. She has conventional ideas of what this should look like. He's off again to America in a day or so and she wants to be proud of him.

"I've found a place straight off, for you, which was a stroke of luck. The Beethovenstrasse, that's very suitable." The 'Musicians' Quarter' is at the flossy end of bourgeois Strasbourg; of nineteenth-century Germanic facture, pompous but of solid worth and weight. Well regarded by the medical profession, which is really why there is an instant barrage of objection and complaint, perturbing Silvia not at all.

"This will go like the hot-cross-buns so I've accepted and I don't want you putting in a veto." Raymond gave her a bloodshot look: bossyboots woman, one shouldn't allow this. So she gave the nail a tap with her hammer.

"I've looked it over, very nice consulting space, came up suddenly, was a cardiologist who suddenly dropped dead."

"The way they do."

"Quite so, it's in tiptop condition and you can keep the cleaning-woman and everything."

"And the large doses of nitroglycerine." He's well aware of being jockeyed.

"Nice little apartment at the back, just right for you on your own. Love-nest, probably." That might have been going too far, but he only stared glassily. Oh yes, that WAS an inducement.

"Good soundproof old building," went on Silvia hurriedly, "sunny behind. Insurance at street level, a gynaecologist on the floor above, it's a snip. I must clinch it before midday, everyone's after it."

"Far too expensive," said Raymond feebly.

"Stop talking bloody nonsense. Money comes to money. You've a patient next week referred by Dr Vincent in Nancy – you must realize, you're on your way." And because it is the moment to change the subject – "There's a flood of e-mail from the people in Oakland about the symposium; oh yes and a new rat joke."

"Oh all right, make the call then, and lets' see the new joke."

Rat jokes – they are in fact lawyer-jokes – have been around a long time. Originally it had been noticed that 'rats and lawyers have much in common. Dishonesty, treachery, and uncontrolled proliferation.' The corridors of the Internet swarm with hordes of lawyers looking like rats – 'Watch out; they gnaw the cables'. In the Research Institutes of the world the standard joke, from which the others flow, had been, 'Why do laboratories use lawyers for experiment?' There are three standard answers: 'There are more lawyers; the lab assistant doesn't get fond of them; there are some things which a rat will simply refuse to do. . .' There is no sign of this slackening, especially after a lawyer has sent in his little bill.

'Dear Colleague, it has for long been known that metamorphosis techniques are freely used: masquerading lawyers indistinguishable from real rats. Metempsychosis now flourishes; the souls of our lawyers' granddams no longer inhabit birds.

'It has recently been signalled that a group of lawyers in the Vatican practises religious discrimination, headed by a gifted swifty, known as Cardinal-Rat. They hand out certificates of conformity, guaranteeing the holder to be a genuine Catholic rat in good standing, backed by the threat that all rats of other persuasions are to be cast out of the community.

'You should place all rats in your laboratory under close surveillance, to determine whether infection is present, not only the familiar phenomenon of rats fluent in legal terminology. Pay particular attention to those with a claim to be orthodox Christian rats (present concern is not so much with Muslim or Jewish rats), especially those wearing ostentatious insignia, showing signs of zealous observance, or otherwise recognizable as engaged in this crusade to eliminate all but true believers. The Cardinal Rat, recognizable by extreme attachment to legal formulae, is said to be active in the Federal Republic, and if seen should be placed in strict isolation.'

"I don't get it," said Silvia. Raymond did though – grinning. His Distinguished Eminence, Cardinal Ratzinger, has been voluble lately about the True Church: Protestants need not apply. As a Jesuit Raymond is always suspect in scientific circles; we have a bad name for legalistic hair-splitting. The bare word 'jesuitical' is automatically pejorative. Too many of us are over-pally with the extreme right wing of clerical reaction, Opus Dei and the like – some indeed downright fascist. Going to America for the symposium, Doctor Valdez is going to get a lot of humour, some of it edgy, fired at him. Respected colleagues, some of them close friends, intensely sensitive about the death penalty or putting icecubes in the cognac, are looking to draw blood elsewhere.

Raymond's research work, involving many rats and likely to involve a good many company lawyers, has been relatively peaceable, on the lines of chemical additives to food – a subject that attracts lawyers. Of recent months, a bit more Iatrogenic in quality: a witch-word this, with which medical jargon makes play, confident nobody will understand it. Roughly, there are medical treatments which, of course quite unintentionally, can contribute to the very affliction they are thought to help prevent. He's aware of being on thin ice here. There are as many cancer-jokes, in the trade, as there are lawyer-jokes.

After sharing it with the immediate colleagues – 'Watch out for any rats wearing Lourdes medals or who tend to get in a corner to recite their rosary' – he went to see Paul the historian, his Companion in Jesus.

"Paul, where is it you get these marvellous cigars?"

"Well my dear, if I told you they are a personal tribute from Fidel you'd not believe me, though we're friends come to that; much abused man, great deal of good in him. I'll give you an anecdote instead of the '14 war, on which as you know I'm thought an authority; the before-and-after are both of great interest. I believe it was in

Ypres that a group of English soldiers living in great misery found themselves surrounded and their officer handed round a parcel of very good cigars he'd saved for a rainy day. When the Germans lined them up outside they were smoking these wonderful things, to the edification of all present. My own attitude is comparable. It's raining outside, I believe," pretending to look. "You wouldn't come to see me unless you were contemplating surrender." So that Raymond told him about the Janeites and their wartime origins.

"Very good," said Paul. "Like all good jokes, true at the core, compare these lawyers of yours, especially the Pious lawyers, who go to Mass daily.

"I'm going to give you a telling-off, because you're a good doctor even when you behave like an imbecile, puffed up as you are with vanity and floundering about like a – but that's what we all are, *pas vrai?* – dolphins, and we get caught and strangled in those abominable nets. Thrashing about, trying hard, knowing ourselves doomed. I don't know your Jane. English humour saves us pretty often. Did it work, d'you think, with your man?"

"To some extent. Who can say more? Early days as yet. We had a friend in common, old French politician we greatly liked, corrupt old man, very clever, immensely amusing. Strong on literature and that gave me the idea. Here we have a disciplined man, highly trained, magnificent physique, remarkable qualities, and just as in 1917 – what a waste! In my story the only survivor is a big strong chap who's been shell-shocked into half-witted numbness and the only reality he can catch hold of is Jane, the little old woman who'd written a few books a hundred years before. Extraordinary books – she discards everything bar the moral essentials which now appear trivial. The group builds them into a standing joke, not altogether cynical because they all know they'll be killed. Only this is worth holding to."

Paul is a good, quiet listener.

"Who is it that has let everyone down? – it's myself. I fell in love with this man's wife. And she with me, I'm afraid. But she has gathered the courage and the honour to cut me off. And this has left me in despair."

"Where did she go?"

"Back to her man; where else would she go?" crossly. "This trap has sharp teeth. Lord, Thou hast made this world but the shadow of a dream." Paul took the ash off his cigar.

"This self-loathing that has overcome you is an unattractive trait. To indulge in anguish and contempt for yourself is consequent upon your contempt of the world, and that's indefensible, as you well know. That the world frightens, appals or revolts is common form. Since the Lord you're making free with gave himself trouble and suffering to redeem it, we must not have the insolence to despise it; that's bad theology. As a doctor you are called upon to combat pain and misery: you swore, I believe, an oath to that effect. To hate the world is to increase misery; that shows you bad at your job.

"Your private life is no concern of mine – help yourself to some whisky my dear, forgive my negligence – but I can't have you doing your job badly; that's pride as well as vanity. Your pettifogging adulteries are of no interest at all but they make you suffer. You shot the albatross and now you have it round your neck. It was a living thing of great beauty and now it's a horrible carcass stinking of bad fish. Your job is to heal wounds, not to make more. From what you tell me your young woman has defied the world and nobly. You may be called upon to do something more, I cannot know, before the albatross is finished with.

"Mustn't feel contempt. Don't belittle your skills. Even if it's only prolonging a life, making an existence tolerable, restoring hope, increasing comfort. And then of course the man you heal goes out and steals from the poor, but that's no concern of yours."

"Fuck you, Paul."

"Have some more whisky."

Monsieur Philippe wasn't happy at all. Gone to a lot of trouble for a good satisfying vengeance, and it fizzles, and now where are you? Even the local paper had been discouragingly meagre. Where he had counted on a gaudy headline, much rhetorical flourish, excitable speculation, outrage; a dry little five-line account headed 'Explosives Attempt' and having the mayor shout about 'cowardly, stupid and

irresponsible' – he said exactly the same about boys throwing stones:
a poor show. 'Considerable damage to the building exterior' is meaningless. Corsicans busting a rural tax-office get a much better outcry.
(He hadn't realized that the local mayor was Geoffrey de Saint-Anne,
who had 'had a word' with the editor.) No better than a tickle.

As is the way with a tickle one has to scratch it in the end.
Monsieur Philippe was not able to resist going to see for himself.
Prudently holding to the top of the slope and peeking across; an
overcast night, too, but there wasn't much to see. That fancy stair-
way to the balcony was gone; some sagging masonry supported by
builders' jacks and the windows boarded up; garage door demol-
ished – yes and no Porsche inside neither; had that gone? A result,
but he'd hoped for much better. Bitched, really. Most of the blast
had gone outward and been wasted.

It had been Geoffrey's suggestion to have a dog 'in case of
prowlers'. William is not dog-minded: 'They bark for nothing at all.'
Nor is Joséphine doggy: vague memory of Sherlock Holmes. 'They
do nothing in the night-time as is well known.' However, Geoffrey
produced the dog. Sleeping at the back (dog in the kitchen). William
noticed nothing until she poked him.

"It's growling." So it was; and walking about; and bristling. One
couldn't see much, out of those front windows. No movement, or if
there was it was gone now. He got a torch and had a tour: nothing.
Dog had quietened now anyway.

Still, in the morning when he let the dog out he went out with it.
Ingrained habit of observation. Well maybe, or maybe not, but security types have the verification habit too, so he went back for a
camera and a measuring tape. Didn't amount to much but there had
been enough of a shower yesterday to tell fresh from old. And the
dog had growled in the night-time. It would do no harm to verify a
bit further. Most of cop-instinct is experience.

"Ho," said Xavier. "You again. Retired, but now a rent-a-cop."
Scrabbling among his papers. "We've had a gendarmerie report. . .
'Affair of stolen gas-tank' – I love that. 'The village supply is held in
the shed. Large impressive padlock but easily opened.' Mm, interrogation. Long confused tale about a half-empty one."

"There's a big hire-deposit charge on those cylinders."

"Right; that's how the shopkeeper noticed. Fella took it by mistake?"

"Would account for the damage being minor, maybe."

Reading from his page – "'The inbreaker knew his way about the village but it is suggested, no longer lives there' – Their conclusion."

"Village people know a full cylinder by the weight. Townspeople might not – My conclusion."

"Now just supposing this geezer you fancy. . . we'll have a go at these photos, might well tell us the type of car."

"Turning out to be the widest-sold Renault on the market."

"Nor is it evidence one could bring in to court: photos could have been made at any time."

"I'm dubious about this theory anyhow. He wouldn't know about the village, wouldn't know where to look. He'd know how to open a lock but I don't see him up there at all."

"He may have an accomplice. Like who bashed your friend Doctor Valdez. We never saw the jeweller for that. But supposing we postulate someone familiar with that village and who got that gas-tank for him?"

"And knew it was half empty?"

"And thought maybe, fella won't know the difference."

Monsieur Philippe was also fishing. One has to persevere. A dud at one end of the pool; try the other. There was something to be made of these people. They were behaving in a funny way. Here in the town one didn't see the woman around: certainty she was no longer living with the doctor, and he too had changed his habits. New car – rather sharp: nice little BMW. Didn't go with the life style. And yes, seems to be planning a move; pricy building in the Musicians' Quarter. What was going on? Hadn't changed jobs; still that old bicycle to go to the research place.

Mr Cleverdick Barton – even knowing his name still thought of as Le Parisien, and a slyboots – was an enigma. One couldn't follow him about: nothing absent-minded about that one. A cop undoubtedly; evident since that unpleasantly jarring encounter. Never seemed to go to work; had been ill judging by the doctor's visits, but now? The village gossip was that the Sainte-Anne woman had been married to him and ho, had gone back to live with him afresh, by all accounts. What now was the story with the doctor?

The explosion had been a flash in the pan. He'd seen as much: windows broken, a few shutters torn off, builders busy with those steps. Chewed the place up a bit, but not good enough. The tormenting taste of salt in the mouth was still there and would stay, until he got this account levelled.

How to get at the slippery bastard? Monsieur Philippe has lost faith in direct action. He preferred to arrange for people to trip themselves up. How about a letter? A technique he has used in business; you plant a few suggestions, which work in the mind. And the fellow might well do something silly. 'Do you think of that doctor as a friend of yours? Or your wife? They are still screwing on the sly. You ought to wake up.' On those lines. Three or four of those, the cat's in with the pigeons. Complaisant husbands are not infrequent but if the fellow gets the idea he's being made a fool of. . . One wants the bastard to squirm.

I've brought this on myself, thought William. A '*corbeau*'. Poison-pen letters in France come from a crow; a cunning bird. Sharp-eyed and slippery; easy to think of it busy writing this sort of stuff. It was of course the same man. He had ridiculed, humiliated that man in his own place. He knew he'd made a bad mistake, overplaying. He'd been angered, and had surrendered to anger. That man had been behind a sneaking attack on my friend, who had been badly hurt. The mechanisms by which this came about weren't of great interest; in the past he'd known other nasty stories with the same kind of motive: the simpleton Janine was at the bottom of it, playing the call-girl. Think herself lucky if punishment hadn't come her way. He'd known girls thrown out of moving cars for overstepping the bounds allowed them: she had some protector, no doubt.

This little man was still trying to get at him, and now through Joséphine; had been spying about, keyholing, it was obvious. Ray was at risk too – but he had to control himself, to protect two people he loved. . . with any luck at all, Xavier would tie this sneak up, and with a ribbon round it. Pah, though; it had spoilt his day. A crow, winking and grinning, and writing little notes.

In the course of a hunt for a telephone number that she was quite sure she had written on the back of an envelope which had disappeared, Joséphine was head down in the wastepaper bucket; simple as that, all among this week's promotions for the supermarket and the impassioned invitations to subscribe to things: poor postman, trudging under the weight of so much Passion. First she sat up, then stood up. William wouldn't be bothered burning such things, or hiding them from her. Wouldn't be framing them to hang on the wall, either: in with the rest of the junk mail. Whoever did that would be careful with fingerprints, or even those handy fragments of DNA we're always told about. Saliva under the stamp, or the lick of the envelope? It didn't have enough importance, even as a piece of evidence to put on a courtroom table.

True, she said "Oh, Shit" but that is not an Impassioned sort of expletive.

If people say I'm a whore, does that make me one? If people think of me as a whore, it's no worse than I deserve. I want to be a woman: it's high time, I have wasted a lot of years. The world is full of women. Some are whores, some are squaws, being Helpmeet to Hubby. Lots trudge after the donkey with a load on their head: their man is riding the donkey, smoking a cigarette and wearing new shoes. Some are power-hungry, go to work and keep slaves. Around here, nearly all are doing jobs, mostly pretty menial; often at half the money a man would be getting. They carry, a great many, an impossible burden; a day's work and then rush, to do the shopping and pick the brats up from the crèche and even then they aren't through: cooking and housekeeping and making a Home for the man and the children. I'll do that if it's what it takes to have self-respect and a straight back. Of these many get abandoned, divorced, pushed out to cope for themselves. Then you have to set up as a single parent, or go lez, along with some other poor cow, it's to be hoped they find some comfort in one another.

But since I'm a woman I have to Be a woman, make a proper job of it. Too many years have gone, lost in being an object.

I hope, thought Joséphine, I have a daughter. Teaching her I'll learn; we'll learn about being women together. a life-time's work, that. Fucking Hard work. And since it's my work get on with it then, stop chatting about it.

Medicine – using the word loosely – proliferates. By a sort of Parkinson Law; there are a lot of inventions, clever mechanical tools, aids to diagnosis or in pointing out a likely treatment. Hospitals yell for more scanners, expensive toys of the sort, because everybody wants to be scanned. Doctors get into the habit of ordering tests; it pleases the patient, who has a comforting feeling of being looked after. You might anyhow find out something you hadn't known before. One of the most frequent tools is the analysis laboratory, since haematologists find more, and more complex questions to ask of a drop of blood. The lab is like a shop on the main road, where everyone pops in to buy a bunch of flowers, so that the one on the Allée de la Robertsau does a roaring trade. Most of the work is boring counts of the banal levels in your blood like cholesterol, but the waiting-room is full of apathetic folk looking for the vampire-girls to call their name and fill the little bottle; rows and rows of these with enough of the stuff to Paint the Town Red.

The Permanent Representative wasn't happy; all much too public for his liking. Nobody knew or cared who he was; neither the paper-work girl at the counter, shuffling her forms, nor the technician with her bright smile and roll-up-your-sleeve. She doesn't even look at your face, sees only your elbow; make a fist then, so that the vein is apparent. But he's always sensitive; however banal the intervention it's an invasion of his privacy, and how can one be sure there's nobody around who might recognize him. He had insisted on Crystal coming with him. It wasn't a smokescreen, nor a comfort; it was a little treat for immediately afterwards. These damn blood tests are always before breakfast, so that he had planned to have her drive him across to the Hilton or wherever, have her pour out the coffee; order a good American breakfast which he never got at home.

Crystal didn't care. She liked this role; it was being a sort of confidante rather than a playmate. She liked soothing him, pouring out the coffee, liked the idea of being posh too; cinnamon toast or something, yum.

Doctor Valdez, sorry sorry, was in a mighty hurry. Off to the farflung today, and cross because he hasn't a direct flight out of Strasbourg; It's Frankfurt OR Paris OR Zürich, hellholes all three. AND a change in Atlanta; why couldn't we have gone to Miami? – yes yes but we've Been to Miami.

Hurry because of being conscientious: he has to give a phonecall to a colleague about a patient's tests and the lab is always slow with the results, so he is going to whip in, pick them up, leaving the car doubleparked and Too Bad. And there on the pavement in front is Dr Barbour. That is all right. A professional discretion obtains, and they won't even nod to each other. But there, holding his arm in a maternal manner is a woman – and that is Janine. He hasn't laid eyes on her since – but oh dear, Janine who has never kept her lip buttoned since the day she was born.

"Ray!" she screamed, delighted.

"Hallo Janine. Look, forgive, I'm dashing, can't stop." She wasn't listening; she never had.

"But Ray, how lovely! You're looking splendid."

"Good to see you, sorry, the police will be giving me a ticket." She was standing there staring after him, puzzled. . .

Dr Barbour is much too self-controlled to make a scene in public. 'In public' – right there on the main road, what a setting for a scandal.

"Get in the car," he said softly. Hers, the little red one, smallest car he'd ever got his legs into. "Drive home. . ."

"Make coffee." Not the breakfast he'd been looking forward to. Interrogation. Soft-voiced and lawyerly. A clumsy liar.

"But nobody could possibly have seen. . ."

Somebody in fact had. Monsieur Philippe simply delighted. And all free, all without effort. He'd been going about his own business, had simply stopped for the red light. A chocolate with a cherry inside. Luscious that little passage on the pavement which one

couldn't hear but the body-language told all. Valdez' car there block-
ing the traffic, and that little old thing of Mireille, Italian racing red.
This would work nicely, would make for a valuable bit of leverage.
That tall figure was unmistakable, the smooth silver hair, it set off
the oddly bleached look of the face – and the way he took her by the
arm. . . rubbing it and you could see the words 'You're hurting'. . .
it was the piece in the puzzle he'd never been sure of; that the Permanent Representative had not known who Dr Valdez was, had
never identified his girlfriend's former playmate. It would be typical
of old-mother-Ben to pretend she didn't know. While knowing perfectly well and blandly instructing himself to get out there and find
out. That was how she worked, staying away from anything likely to
be troublesome. Yo – this was a handy thing to know.

Dr Barbour sat at his desk. The house was quiet. The staff had
gone home; Eleanor was out playing bridge; the houseman had the
day off. He would drive himself, later, to – whatever it was, it would
be in the diary. He likes this quiet hour before going up to change.
By the door the little telltale told him that the security was on. He'd
have said, up to yesterday, that his own was reliable. Anonymous
letters, such as everyone in official positions must get from time to
time, would never interfere, he had supposed, with the ability to
think clearly. In a lawyerlike manner.

He put his finger inside the triggerguard and twirled the gun on
the desk. It pointed towards him. No. Try again. It pointed towards
the door.

It lived in his desk, which nobody touches. Of European make but
said to be good, a stopper, powerful. It is our constitutional right, to
bear arms. He had never taken it out but it was there, carefully kept
oiled, with the charger separate to avoid weakening the spring. The
armourer had explained; light enough for him but efficient, an automatic known here as a seven-six-five. He knew how to snap it in, to
arm the action, feeling for the safety but now it was loaded, a fer-de-
lance ready to strike.

He had got the story out of Crystal with no trouble at all; a stupid
confusion of names. Calling herself Mireille and her real name was
Janine. Harmless, a thing actors did. But this doctor made nonsense

of safeguards. The man had been here in this room, questioning him, examining him. Prescribed for him. He had inner uncertainties, which now were known to this man, who was due – away at some conference, in the States – to come back with the result of those lab tests, and discuss a possible treatment. . . it doesn't bear thinking of. It is like a bullet, lodged in the centre of his own bodily defences. A lawyer is a man. His blood is red.

It is true, one thinks of lawyers as cold, implacable, unmoved; Mr Tulkinghorn at his desk with the two bits of sealing-wax and the broken glass stopper. Men can be overwhelmed by pain and by a pressure suddenly unbearable. They can run amok; the head no longer controls the heart, the limbs, the armed hand. But not, one would say, lawyers: still less those who represent their country on diplomatic missions, clothed as it were in the Advocate-General's red robe. People like this shouldn't have loaded pistols on the table.

But it would be very foolish to think of somebody like Dr Barbour in an over-simplified, caricatural way. He is imbued with a sense of his importance? He is pompous, rigid, humourless? Authoritarian, a bully, a good deal of an old fascist? One would still know pitifully little about him. Raymond Valdez is thinking about how one will get to know more, and maybe, enough to be of some use. This will take time, effort, concentration, sympathy. The PermRep is a lot of boilerplate: there is much more to him. He is to a large degree a creature of systems and attitudes and the conventions of his class and upbringing. He is also – as he is telling himself – red-blooded. He lives and he breathes, and he loves. He is making indeed a great effort to be a man. Not to be mechanical, materialist. The pistol is a well-made ingenious mechanism but it means death. It is not a piece of sealing-wax. The Permanent Representative took it to pieces again and put it back in the drawer, after ejecting the loaded cartridge. It left a smell of mineral oil on his hands, so that he went to wash before going up to change. Not Spaniards – New Zealand. Mutton probably, or apples.

This evening the catering is by the Bénédicte firm. She does none of the big parties, boumboum affairs with hundreds of plates and glasses, but is in much demand for a more intimate affray. She has an excellent maître d'hôtel and two inventive cooks, and the secret is to have a personal eye upon the lay-out. Dr Barbour filtered through the *convives*.

"Two words with you."

"With pleasure," one eye on a waitress. "Careful dear, those are delicate." She doesn't disdain what cooks call the chicken-and-ham circuit but they aren't sausage rolls: Canapé MacMahon is a short-crust tartlet with scalloped chicken livers, mushrooms and marrow; a madeira demiglace.

"I've had a piece of insolence from an employee of yours."

"You may rely on me to deal with it."

The phonecall had said nothing beyond 'I want to see you' but Monsieur Philippe doesn't loiter, pausing only downstairs where there is a nice smell of fresh pastry and a gamy flavour from the kitchen beyond. The old horror's office was upstairs. She doesn't say Good Morning, she doesn't ask him to sit down, she's plainly in a nasty frame of mind.

"You were employed some months ago on an errand for a valued customer. It now appears that you have exceeded your instructions: a complaint has come in. You've pestered him, you've been indiscreet. Trying to make yourself a corner in the affairs of others. I won't have it." Reading him off as though he'd dropped a tray of glasses but he will bide his time. "You need not speak, I won't listen. You need only understand me – you haven't heard the last of this."

"I don't allow you to make threats."

"I never make threats. I dislike complaints, they're bad for business. I know how to put a stop to them, get that well fixed in your mind. Off you trot; I'm wanted downstairs."

Talking to me like that – that you'll regret, old bitch. Not the moment to say so and it needs quiet, collected thought. Now he had to go down the stairs in front of her, as though pushed. . .

She was buttonholed in the hallway by a distraught waitress.

"Oh Madame, James says the delivery has gone wrong." She bullocked on through without a backward glance and Monsieur Philippe had a sudden inspiration, whipped back up the stairs three at a time. Anything, anything at all – a paper, a tape cassette? The desk was bare, the drawers all locked – cow. Only on the window-sill, a cigarbox. To offer favoured customers or might it hold a recorder? Well Glory Be. It held a small pistol. He slipped back down silent as the draught from an open door, ready to say Sorry, forgotten my glasses, but there was nobody at all. He didn't know what one could make of this but something – something.

At home he examined the booty. A woman's thing yes, but trust old Benny, no Mickey Mouse. A small but solid, shapely job, revolver loaded all round with .22 magnums. . .

It might be some time before she missed it. It might not be such an obvious guess who had found it. She wouldn't do anything at once. She had, no error, leverage on him, but he, if she pushed too far, could find a few damaging suggestions. Neither party would be enthusiastic for a shakedown. Say nothing, keep it safe.

He had no gun, himself, since that damned impudent Barton had taken his, chucked it in the river. He'd been meaning to replace it but hadn't found the right opening.

It was at this moment that he found the germ – the faintest shadow – of what looked like a bright idea. A wild plan, but simple. 'Doctor Valdez' he told himself sarcastically, would be part of this. The weak link, the way in. The more he thought, the thirstier he got.

But Valdez seemed to have vanished; no sign of him at either address. He rang up the secretary, an earnest enquirer, quite humble and prepared to wait upon the convenience of almost anyone but he did want, you see. Oh, he was away? But he'd be back on Friday? Oh yes, I see, the timeshift from the States. I wouldn't want to bother him, it would be better to wait until Monday perhaps.

He had what he wanted, the plane timetable.

Yawning exaggeratedly, waiting for his ears to clear, Raymond doesn't object to the tropic climes now and then but he does like to get home to where it rains, or might, outside; oh god why do these places stink so and why is my suitcase always the last one off? Caribbean islands fade to postcard size, mercifully cleansed of insects, air conditioners and penetrating American voices. And now dozy is the word and he has a horrible longing for soup. Pea soup and no bananas. Where the buggery is one to find soup? Minestrone.

It is needlessly dozy to be looking in the car park for an old Volkswagen. He has a smart new car and a magic thingy to pop the doors, if one could find it. . . The man next door is hunting for his key which isn't in his pocket and might be in the briefcase, well one knows the feeling. Throwing his bag in the back he was suddenly crowded.

"Stay very still, there's a pistol pointing at you. Now I get in, just behind you. No use staring about, those cars are all empty, gone to Paris for the day. Now if you turn your head slowly you'll see it. Small but efficient. The target would be the back of your neck and you're dead.

"Now you drive out slowly, careful not to hit anything. Got the money, have you, to make the gate open and get us out of here?"

Supposing I haven't any money, thought Raymond, the gate won't open. Only this is airport desert, everyone else is gone, even the taxi-drivers are miles away sunk in a doze; lift your eyes from the cross-word, boys. No, I'm stuck here with a maniac just behind me and what does he want, what the hell is the point? Why hijack me? Why hijack anyone? Is he escaping from somewhere? Or he's done a holdup and I'm a hostage. Where are the bloody police, are they all inside drinking coffee? It was only a feeder flight. Big plane there coming in and lots of people, no good to me and I don't Want to get shot in the neck.

"Right, now I'll tell you, you drive on out to Barton's house. You know the way well. Where you left your woman, right?"

Light is beginning to dawn and it doesn't help. Being dozy and being frightened together is just making you sweaty. Is this – this must be the man who has some vengeance to take upon William. Who put the bomb outside William's house. Not a very efficient man because it didn't work well, but he might be better with guns than he was with bombs. This is not a good forecast. What can I do, *dio merda*? Tip the car in the ditch, like Joséphine did? Alack, there are country roads hereabout, stretches of woodland, farmland – ditches. But these lands are much too tame, orderly, ditches much too neat and small. Crash the car into something? There are villages with awkward turns, red lights, cars parked. This would be possible. He doesn't think he can do it; too paralysed by fear. You are not that smart, Ray, and you are not that heroic. As he got into the car the first thing the man had done was to make a sudden lunge forward over my shoulder, to twist the reversing mirror up and out of sight-line; didn't want to be seen. That would have been the moment for the unarmed combat; take the loony in the octopus-like grip. I didn't; I did nothing.

Looking backward is of no interest, thought Ray. More anxious to know what is in front. The fiend is just behind me and it's enough to know he's there. 'The fiend is at my elbow' said. . . said. . . Lancelot Gobbo. . . that's me, the clown. This feeling of total impotence is wretched. "Watch your road" snapped the man. "Don't waver. Don't try anything funny."

He could bash the car into a tree. Would that leave them all trapped in airbags? – he doesn't even know how the damn things work. Are there some at the back? And if he fired his pistol into them, wouldn't they collapse?

Sweat is running down his neck, his chest, his back: his trousers were sticking to his legs. He could pee in his pants it wouldn't make much odds. Raymond has practised dying – many times – but he hadn't known it would be like this. And now they were climbing the steep slope, up to the house.

"Easy does it. Nice and slow. At the top you just glide down into the dip. You stop there, in front of the house. And you sound your horn. You go toot-toot. You don't move. And he'll hear that, and he'll come out to see. Think there's something wrong with you. There is, too. He'll come to look, and I've got him, the bastard."

It was all too likely. It was logical. William would think no harm. The one hope – that William, the professionally suspicious man, would think something amiss. He has weaponry, but how to alert him to the need for it? It was all true – William would simply come out wondering what the matter was. Joséphine – she might be there; she might come out too. The loony would not leave an inconvenient witness. They would all die.

"Toot again," said the voice. "Pip-pip, here he comes."

The car was angled towards the house. The back window was sliding down. Raymond slumped. He didn't think he'd be able to see the others die. In the story, after the bombardment, the simple-Simon says 'I was the only Janeite left'. But it won't be that way. We'll all be gone, with nothing to show. There is no one here and this man is going to get clear away with it. He heard the hissing breath drawn in and held as William started to come towards them.

A different voice, barking, wanting to sound gruff, authoritative and wishing very strongly to be obeyed, said loudly,

"Drop the gun."

Of several startled people Monsieur Philippe was the most startled – William, who could see behind Raymond's car, could see the other car which had stopped at the top of the dip, wasn't startled. It meant that Xavier had been as good as his word and put a PJ man sticking to that idiot's footsteps, and just as bloody well because the fucker'd turned dangerous. He caught hold of Joséphine's arm and swung her violently, himself making a complicated sort of plunging swerve. He hoped that boy knew what he was doing.

Melodrama is never far from farce. Raymond with his eyes shut wasn't sure whether he was in this world or the next. Whichever it was, that was a classic line.

Humphrey Bogart always said the line never existed, but that drunks in bars, anxious to show who really was the tough guy around here, were forever coming up to him making like they were George Raft, saying 'Drop the gun, Louey.'

The boy from the PJ – he was not much more – was frightened by the situation and startled at his own voice. There he'd been stuck for hours on end, at that frigging airport, wondering what the hell the bugger was up to – practically since the beginning of his shift. Recognizing Dr Valdez he'd woken up. Followed from fairly far back. They'd gone quite slow. When they stopped he'd known something was up. Training took over then. He'd made quick time while angling out a bit. Because of Valdez in front. If you have to use your piece you try to make sure it doesn't go on through and hit a bystander.

But Monsieur Philippe was very badly startled because it never had occurred to him to look behind him. The window down; he had the little pistol nicely braced, cocked, on single action.

At that wild Indian yell panic struck him. He swung the little gun in that direction and it went off (found afterwards to have a light pull, nothing unusual) and before he knew how to stop fired two more on double action.

The boy had his big standard-issue .357 revolver. There has been a lot of debate about police arms. The thing is dangerously powerful. Most PJ men of more experience have gone back to automatics, for the modern automatic is much more reliable than it used to be. The boy had been trained that if you do have to use your piece (after, it's insisted upon, your call of warning) you shoot at the legs. Nobody'd ever shown him how you're supposed to aim at some geezer sitting down in a car whom you can't even see properly. No matter anyhow, these big guns kick up in the inexperienced hand. One shot but it fair tore the fellow in two and went out the far side. Jeesus-eff-christ, he thought, scared out of his wits. William didn't need a second glance to see what had happened. He took the big revolver away from the boy, who put his hands up over his eyes, and said, "That's all right, son, get your breath back." The boy began to cry from nerves. He'd never fired the gun at anyone and now he'd killed a man. Stopped at once; it was only the scare.

"The ol'man'll tear my head off for this. There'll be an inquiry, I'll be suspended."

"No he won't. Happens I know him, pretty well; he'll take my word. You don't touch any of this. You go back to your car, and call him. You let him shout, and then you tell him Mr Barton will be your witness."

Raymond was still sitting there behind the wheel, clutching it. Joséphine reached in and took both hands.

"Come on. Upsidaisy." He got out, took a look, and said

"Oh dear. My good car." Insane laughter.

"The mirror cracked from side to side. Your insurance company is going to do its nut."

"Not sure I haven't peed my pants."

"Would make two of us. Take a look at William, he's in his element." Raymond tried walking, with partial success.

Joséphine is especially fond of Ray's quickness to laugh at himself. William joined them.

"I had a quick word with Xavier. He'll send the wagon and he'll be out himself for a look before they take – that – away. The boy stays, to be sure no one touches it. I think he'd like a cup of coffee, Joséphine, if you'd manage that. What I'd suggest, we go in, and perhaps we all have some apple pie."

So there they are, the three Janeites.

"Aren't we perfect fools, to imagine we can push violence out of the way? The harder we push, the more it clings."

"Like Captain Haddock" (Joséphine is a strong Tintin fan) "trying to get rid of the sticking-plaster."

"But Haddock's violence is entirely innocent."

"That's what children like so much: they can feel total confidence in him."

"Do you think," said William, "that the jeweller was any good at his job?" The other two have had it explained to them, who the little sneak was.

"Oddly enough," said Joséphine, "I can answer that. I've been in that little shop on the quays. Geoffrey was buying a wedding anniversary present for Liliane. Yes he was. Very good indeed. They aren't all sitting up there in the Place Vendôme, you know. He had a passion for gold. Not that shit stuff – pink, grey, white. The real thing, high carat. You wear that on your skin, it takes a beautiful patina. He learned that, he said, in India. The inside – where it touches you, there is the heart and the soul of it. He did the most wonderful enamels on it. Isn't that beautiful? Why was he such a horrible little shit?"

The PJ chief could be heard outside, brisk, rallying his troops. Xavier came in, said, "What's that you're drinking? I'll have some. . . You all right, all of you?"

"We've a technical question for you."

"Good, this. Polish, is it? I can give you the police answer, if William hasn't already."

"No, I haven't the details."

"I had a man on him, as you know. Just a tag, wasn't getting any-where much with it – interested in the Doctor," nodding at Ray.

"Old bitch Bénédicte came in to see me, bold as brass."

"Her good pistol, which Of Course is legally registered, and was, so please you, mislaid while cleaning, got pilfered. An Insane thing to do, Commissaire, which she feels Obliged to make known to me, think of it, fellow running round with a Grievance.

"Sure; insanity's what they all plead; something came over me donchaknow. No more insane than you are." The three looked at each other. Barking bonkers the lot of us. "Thing is, it's perfectly true, pretty well anybody will do something insane at a given moment, press the sore point hard enough and fellow isn't reasoning clearly. Likely enough, this was the moment, incapable of calculation, pick up the breadknife you've a homicide. This little fellow had been prac-tising his vengeance a long time, sure, tasting it and loving it; seeing the gun there he takes leave of his senses. Afterwards, no no, it wasn't him; was the Third Man. Bit late perhaps for the victim. William, old son, just as well, huh, having that boy there, bit dozy but didn't quite drop all his marbles. All right, mustn't stand here gossiping, thanks for the drink, I better get to work, lot of forms to fill in."

Outside, they were towing away Doctor Valdez' good new car. Raymond helped himself to another socking glassful of apple pie.

"I fell asleep on the plane," he told them. "Girl gives you a pillow but it's probable my head was in a bad position. There's a lot we don't understand about nightmare; it's interesting that it's called Alptraum in German.

"I was driving at night. Maybe I was on an English road, over on the wrong side, because bang, there are headlights blazing right in my face, there was nothing I could do but think This is It. The other driver swerved at the last possible second, I remember hearing him scrape along the bodywork and I still couldn't react – there was another set of lights bearing down on me. I woke, then.

"It was like there in the car; I was in a lather, I rang the bell, sent the girl for a big drink. I'm saying that if it was premonition how do I get it there, in the middle of the ocean?"

The others were saying nothing, looking at him. I'm getting drunk, thought Raymond.

There had been papers lying about: he had picked one up, to obliterate the nasty moment. There was a picture of a piece of sculpture, a big one, monumental. Interview with the artist. Basque, interesting man, said something striking. He wanted to tell the others but his throat was stuck.

'Wouldn't art be the consequence of a necessity to try to do something we don't know how to do?' Indeed; a beautiful, a delicate necessity. . .

It's this apple-pie. He was a student again, arguing with the others; pavement café in Poland. A million years ago, a million miles away. Magali put that record on again. They all played it, all the time; it had become an obsession, there in the heat, the dust.

Not Poland at all. Africa; these hundreds and thousands of black people all looking for help, and we had so little help to give. Magali, the nurse who worked with him; he can see her, a fall of dark hair held in an elastic band. He has cut all his own off; sand gets in it. Magali has a gramophone in the tent.

They all like to sing it, overworked and overtired as they all were. Bass drum, jarring like the springs of the jeep on the iron-hard piste, jouncing them. A prowling rhythm, easy to sing. Magali would begin, and he would join in.

'You'll never know how much I love you.
Never know how much I care. . .'

He was singing it now; didn't care how drunk he was.

Bang went that deep drum. Magali screamed out 'Fever!' That was what it was all about. That was the obsession. 'You get the fever that's so hard to bear. . .' He ought to teach it to these two, who are laughing at him because he's drunk.

Bang went Magali's fist on the table, in time with the drummer. He used to dance with her – a thin, bony thing. Good nurse, though.

He would make these two sing, and dance, along with him.

'Everybody gets the fever.'

Grandfontaine, Christmas 2000

EuroCrime
from Arcadia Books

Nicolas Freeling
Because of the Cats
'One of my favourites' – P.D. James

The Janeites
'A great European novelist' – Francis Wheen

Some Day Tomorrow
'Should have won every literary prize going' – *Literary Review*

The Village Book
'Marvellous' – Anita Brookner, *Spectator*

Eugenio Fuentes
The Depths of the Forest
'Falling in love with a dead woman has never seemed so possible –
or so strange' – Stella Duffy

Jean-Claude Izzo
One Helluva Mess
'A pacy and sharp roman policier' – Boyd Tonkin, *Independent*

Dominique Manotti
Rough Trade
'Extraordinarily vivid' – Joan Smith, *Independent*

Kjersti Scheen
Final Curtain
'Riveting' – *Svenska Dagbladet*

Gunnar Staalesen
The Writing on the Wall
'Murder, violence and lots of sex' – *Birmingham Post*

Richard Zimler
The Last Kabbalist of Lisbon
'An American Umberto Eco' – Francis King, *Spectator*